DEADLY PAYBACK

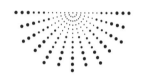

D. S. BUTLER

❀ Created with Vellum

DEADLY PAYBACK

DEADLY PAYBACK is the sixth book in the DS Jack Mackinnon Crime Series.

This time there is no escape…

A literary agent is murdered… A personal trainer lies dead in a car park… What secret connects them?

When a top literary agent's bloated and disfigured body is found in one of London's most prestigious hotels, Detective Sergeant Mackinnon and the rest of MIT get to work. As the body count rises, the team are under pressure to find out what connects the victims.

Who wants these people dead, and why? The truth turns out to be more shocking than anyone expected.

DEADLY PAYBACK is a British police procedural, perfect for fans of Peter James and his Roy Grace detective series.

For Paula

CHAPTER ONE

AT FOURTEEN, I WOULD NEVER have believed I would become a killer.

People think that killers are different somehow, missing that vital component that tells the rest of the population the difference between right and wrong. But that's not true. Up until I was fourteen, I was perfectly normal. Even now, I wasn't what people would expect from a killer.

I don't torture animals. I have a steady job. I love my mother. I like to watch soaps on TV. I'm just like everyone else, except for one thing: I am about to commit murder.

I could still back out, turn around and go home, but even though that thought was there at the back of my mind, I didn't consider it seriously. I'd been waiting for this moment for years. Obsessing, daydreaming, plotting... It had taken over my life.

There was no going back now.

The view from the fifty-second floor of the Shard was

breathtaking. The City of London spread out before me, and I could see the snaking outline of the Thames. I stared at the lights reflected on the river's surface, unable to wrench my eyes away. For a moment, the murmur of voices in the bar seemed to melt into the background as I drank in the view. I'd never seen London from this viewpoint before. It was beautiful.

A voice behind me cut through my thoughts, and I turned around.

I smiled at the barman and reached out a shaky hand to grasp the stem of my champagne glass. I paid him and waited for my change.

I glanced to my left and right, making sure I hadn't attracted any unwanted attention. Sipping on my drink, I tried to relax and fit in. I needed to act normally tonight. Everything depended on it.

I smiled at the barman as he pushed my change towards me, but he barely glanced at me before he moved on to serve the man to my right. And that was a good thing — it was exactly what I wanted.

I surveyed the room. It was busy, but no one was paying attention to me. I grabbed my coat and carried my glass over to a table where I could sit with a view of the entrance.

A loud laugh from a group over by the floor-to-ceiling windows made me jump. They looked like an office group, having an early Christmas party. One of the men wore a Santa hat. I wouldn't have thought that this was the type of place to hold a Christmas party. I guessed they had to be bankers. Or perhaps they worked in insurance. It had to be a job which paid them an obscene amount of money. The cost of drinks here was extortionate.

I looked away and sat down.

She wasn't here yet. I could feel the swell of panic building in my chest. I forced myself to calm down, and took another sip of my champagne, savouring the sensation of bubbles on my tongue. But then I put the glass back on the table. I couldn't drink too much. I needed to keep my wits about me tonight.

Two women drifted past my table, their faces plastered with a ridiculous amount of makeup. I wrinkled my nose at the strong, cloying scent one of them wore. It smelled like cheap air freshener.

I checked my watch. The reception party should be over by now. I'd been so sure she'd come here for a drink afterwards. My whole plan rested on her habits. But it was risky. She might not come to the bar at all. Maybe she'd gone straight back to her room and ordered a drink from room service.

I clenched my fists on my lap. It didn't matter. Either way, she wouldn't escape.

A movement to my right caught my attention, and I inhaled sharply when I saw her.

She wasn't alone. She was with a friend — a man.

I narrowed my eyes as I watched them, glad that the bar was dark and I could sit there unnoticed.

Beverley Madison was petite, blonde and successful. Anyone sitting within ten feet of her would know that because she was taking great delight in loudly telling her male companion just how she had amazed everyone in the industry by creating a bidding war for her client's new book at the book fair today.

To his credit, the man she was talking to didn't yawn

once.

I hadn't been wrong about her drinking. As they chatted, she guzzled down three glasses of champagne. Her companion was still on his first drink.

When she finally drained her third glass, she got up, unsteady on her feet. She scooped up her bag, kissed her friend on both cheeks and headed out of the bar.

I almost smiled in relief when I realised he wasn't going with her. That would definitely make things easier for me.

I wanted to follow her straight away, and it took all my willpower to stay seated at my table by the exit. My hands gripped the edge of the smooth polished wood as I tried to focus my attention on her friend, who remained in the bar. He ordered another drink and asked for his bill.

It was almost time.

I knew from my research the man's name was Barry Henderson. He was a work colleague and had known Beverley for years. He checked his mobile phone, scrolling through the screen.

The minutes passed slowly.

Hurry up, you stupid man. Finish your drink.

Finally, he stood up, dropping a bank note on the table for a tip. As he started to make his way out of the bar, he dialled a number on his mobile phone.

Grabbing my stuff, I followed him. I slipped my arms in the sleeves of my heavy coat and raised the hood.

With my face hidden to the CCTV camera, I smiled as I entered the lift. Barry Henderson still had his phone clamped to his ear and was paying me no attention.

He pushed his hotel key card into the slot and pressed the button for the forty-fourth floor.

He glanced at me then, with a questioning look.

"I need the forty-fourth floor, too," I said and smiled again.

It wasn't an act. It was a genuine smile. Barry Henderson might not realise it yet, but he was helping me. Beverley Madison was about to meet her maker, and I couldn't be happier.

CHAPTER TWO

BEVERLEY MADISON STUMBLED INTO HER hotel room, rubbing her bleary eyes. Hell, it had been a long day! She grinned to herself. A long day and a very successful one, even if she did say so herself.

She had managed to sell some paperback rights to numerous foreign publishers for huge sums of money. Her success had been the talk of the book fair. Beverley had lost count of the number of agents who had come up to offer their congratulations. Of course, secretly they were all envious. They wanted to find out her negotiation secrets. Still, it was nice to have some recognition for all her hard work.

Her smile turned to a scowl as she thought of Jacob Jansen, her top-earning client. He'd been difficult recently. Demanding more and more of her time.

That prima donna was never happy. He thought she should devote all her time to him. He really believed the bloody world should revolve around him. Beverley shook her head as she dumped her handbag on the desk. Writers, they were all the same once they'd had a taste of success. At the start of their careers, they couldn't be more accommodating, but once they started to sell more than a few copies, they went out of their way to be difficult.

Hopefully, this new foreign rights deal should get Jacob Jansen off her back for a little while.

Beverley took a moment to look out of the window. She didn't dare get too close. She'd jumped at the chance to spend the night at the Shard - all expenses paid by Jacob Jansen's German publisher. It was all part of their plan to woo Jansen and secure the publishing rights for his next book. There were positive points to being a literary agent. She enjoyed being wined and dined by publishing companies eager to work with her clients.

But Beverley hated heights, and she shivered at the sight of those tall majestic buildings so far beneath her. She stepped back and turned away from the window.

She unbuttoned her dress, slipping it down her body, and reached into her wheeled designer case for the nightgown. She kicked off her heels at the same time and moaned in relief, flexing her toes.

It really wasn't fair that something so pretty could be so painful, she thought, staring down at her strappy gold sandals. She yawned, picked up her wash bag and started to walk towards the bathroom, when there was a knock at the door.

Beverley gave a huff of annoyance. Who on earth could that be? It better not be room service. She'd been disturbed by room service three times when she'd stayed in Frankfurt last month. It turned out someone had been requesting room service using her room number. Some pathetic joke from someone who was jealous of Beverley's success. She never did find out who had been behind it though.

She strode across the room, determined to give whoever was knocking at the door a piece of her mind, but when she yanked open the door, the reprimand died on her lips.

The person standing in the doorway was definitely not from the hotel.

She blinked at the hooded figure. *What on earth?*

"What do you want?"

Beverley waited a moment but the person at the door didn't reply. She didn't have the patience for this. She was tired. It had been a long day and she just wanted to curl up in bed. Already, she could feel the start of a headache brewing, a sign that a hangover would not be far off. Just thinking of all the paperwork she had to do tomorrow, writing up all the negotiation notes made her head spin.

"What is it?" she snapped and put her hand on the door ready to slam it shut.

It didn't occur to her to be afraid. It was a five-star hotel and people would hear if she shouted for help. Only a fool would try something here.

Beverley frowned. This had better not be another aspiring writer. People wouldn't believe how some writers picked the most ridiculous moments to pitch their work. A writer had once cornered her in the ladies' room at the Frankfurt book fair. Honestly, when would they learn that there was an appropriate time and place to approach an agent.

The figure stayed silent, just lifted their head a fraction.

Beverley shivered. *Creepy weirdo.*

She grabbed the door and shoved it, but it didn't slam shut because the figure blocked it with their foot.

Beverley's eyes widened, and she stepped back. "How dare you. Get out!"

She'd meant to sound commanding and strong, but the voice that left her mouth was almost strangled with fear, not quite a scream, but high-pitched and reedy.

I stepped forward into the hotel room. I'm not really sure how I expected Beverley to respond. I think I wanted her to recognise me. But there had been no recognition in her eyes, only irritation, at first.

Now, her initial irritation had turned to fear.

"Calm down," I said, closing the door behind me.

But Beverley had no intention of calming down. In her scramble to get away from me, she knocked over a chair and tripped, sending the lamp on the desk crashing to the floor.

I stayed rooted to the spot and raised my hands with my palms up. "Keep calm," I said. "I only want to talk."

"Get out of my room! How dare you barge in here like this!"

I took another step forward. My whole plan depended on being able to get close to her. But it wasn't working.

At the worst possible moment, my hood fell backwards, revealing my face. For a brief moment, Beverley hesitated in confusion, and then she let out an almighty scream.

But it was not because she recognised my face.

She screamed because she saw the item I pulled out of my pocket.

I was already wearing my protective gloves, but I still needed to be careful. One slip and it would all be over.

I pulled off the cap of the hypodermic needle and held up the small syringe.

I made a quick movement towards her, and Beverley dived over the mattress, pulling off the sheets as she slid to the floor on the other side of the bed.

She flattened her body against the glass windows and screeched again. "Why are you doing this? Please stop."

She was backed up against the window and had nowhere else to go. I leaned forward, and with a quick movement, I jabbed the syringe in her neck and pushed down the plunger.

Just as quickly, I withdrew the needle. It was all over in seconds.

I smiled at her. "It was just a scratch," I said. "There now, that wasn't so bad, was it?"

The glass squeaked as Beverley Madison slid down the window, and she landed on her backside with a thud.

"All that fuss over nothing." I smiled down at her.

I hoped to God the rooms were well-insulated. I hadn't expected her to freak out so quickly. It was my first time, so mistakes were to be expected.

"What was that? What have you done to me? You won't get away with this." Beverley hugged her knees to her chest, cowering away from me.

"Perhaps not," I said, slipping the cap back on the syringe and sitting down on the edge of the bed. "But it will still be worth it."

"Please let me go," she said slowly. It could have been my imagination, but I thought she was already slurring her words. Of course, that could have been the alcohol.

"I can give you money…" Beverley said, fixing me with her pleading eyes.

"No, money isn't what I need."

"What then? What is it you want?" Beverley held a hand to her neck and winced.

"I don't want much," I said. "Just a little chat."

CHAPTER THREE

DETECTIVE SERGEANT JACK MACKINNON PULLED up outside the entrance to the hotel on St Thomas Street. The street was blocked by marked police cars, and the front of the hotel was cordoned off with blue and white tape. A group of uniforms stood next to the revolving door at the entrance, checking people entering and leaving the hotel.

Crowds of tourists were gathered by the tape, gawping and gossiping about what had happened. An incident like this wasn't good for the city's reputation. Mackinnon knew the senior investigating officer would already be feeling the pressure.

Mackinnon showed his warrant card to the young officer standing by the police tape and signed the paperwork.

"The crime scene is on the forty-fourth floor, sir."

"Who is up there?"

"DI Tyler, sir. DCI Brookbank is the SIO. It's a nasty one. The body has blown up like a balloon, I heard."

Mackinnon thanked him and took a deep breath as he walked towards the entrance.

He stepped inside one of the elevators at the back of the lobby, and less than twenty seconds later, Mackinnon stepped out onto the forty-fourth floor of the Shard.

Another uniformed officer waved him towards a hotel room the police were using as a hub, and Mackinnon quickly changed into a too-small, uncomfortable, blue protective oversuit and matching overshoes.

He followed the trail of police activity to the crime scene and met DI Tyler at the door.

DI Tyler had his grey hair slicked back, revealing his large forehead, which was creased into a perpetual frown. Tyler looked up at Mackinnon, and the corner of his mouth raised into a half-hearted smile.

"Couldn't find one to fit, Jack?"

"Oh, sure. I just thought cropped trousers were in this season."

Tyler smirked. "You look ridiculous."

"Thanks. What have we got?" Mackinnon asked with some trepidation. Tyler's face looked more drawn than usual. The lines around his mouth were pronounced as he set his lips in a firm line.

Tyler glanced back inside the hotel room, then said, "Our victim was Beverley Madison, a high-flying literary agent. Thirty-nine years old. Single. She lived in St. John's Wood, but she spent the night here after some kind of book fair gathering last night."

"Why would she stay here if she's got her own place in London?"

Tyler shrugged. "Pricey hotel, very luxurious. I live in Clapham, but I wouldn't turn down a night here if someone else was footing the bill. She probably put it on expenses."

Mackinnon stepped inside the door, making sure he kept to the marked area. The crime scene officers were just finishing up.

"Who found her?"

"One of the hotel under managers, this morning. The hotel said she didn't respond to her wake-up call, and she didn't answer room service when they brought her breakfast, so they came to check on her. They found her lying over there by the window." Tyler pointed.

There were smears on the glass, but beyond there was a beautiful view of London stretched out for miles.

"They've taken the body away already," Mackinnon said, stating the obvious.

"Yes. Be thankful you didn't see her. She was swollen up. Hideous. I've never seen anything like it."

Tyler called over one of the crime scene photographers and took the man's camera. He flicked through the digital images so Mackinnon could see Beverley Madison's body.

Mackinnon felt his stomach clench as he took a long hard look at the images. There was only a small amount of dried blood on her forehead, but her whole face was swollen and purple.

"Where's the blood from?"

"We think she hit her head against the window." Tyler nodded at the blood smear on the glass.

"Was that the cause of death?" Mackinnon asked. "And

what on earth would cause her to bloat up like that? Some kind of post-mortem reaction?"

Tyler shrugged. "No idea yet. The duty pathologist suggested an allergic reaction, but we won't know any more until after the post-mortem."

"Do we have a time of death yet?"

"Nothing precise," Tyler said. "But either late last night or the early hours of this morning."

Mackinnon exhaled a long breath. That didn't narrow it down much, and they had a whole hotel full of potential suspects.

He stared down at the camera again. Looking at a murder victim was never an easy thing to do, but this one was something else. It was in another league altogether.

"Here," Tyler said, thrusting the victim's driving licence, enclosed in an evidence bag, in front of Mackinnon. "That's what she looked like before."

Mackinnon could scarcely believe it was the same woman. She had large intelligent eyes, high cheekbones and had worn her hair in a blonde bob.

"Hell of a difference, right?"

Mackinnon nodded. "When was the last time anyone saw her?"

"At the bar last night, at eleven pm. There's CCTV in most of the corridors and in the lifts. I've got DC Collins looking into that."

Mackinnon nodded, still staring at the bloated corpse of Beverley Madison. She was still wearing her jewellery, and the swollen flesh on her fingers had curved around a gold band. It looked incredibly painful, but of course at the time the photograph was taken, Beverley Madison wouldn't have been able to feel a thing. Had her body swollen up before she died? Perhaps her swollen fingers had stopped the killer removing the ring.

"They didn't take her ring," Mackinnon said.

"Yes, I think we can rule out robbery. Nothing was taken, as far as we can tell. Cash and bank cards were still in her purse, inside a designer handbag. She still has all her jewellery, including a diamond bracelet that looks like it was worth a few bob."

"If it wasn't a robbery, are we looking at a sex crime?"

Tyler shook his head. "Can't rule it out until after the post-mortem, but there's no evidence of that either."

Mackinnon frowned and handed the camera back to the photographer. "What do you need me to do?"

"First off, find Collins and make sure he's okay with the CCTV, and then we'll head back for the briefing at nine am. DCI Brookbank is the senior investigating officer on this one, but I'm taking the briefing. We will assign actions then, okay?"

Mackinnon nodded and took a last look at the opulent hotel suite. The dominating feature was the huge floor-to-ceiling windows, opening up onto a spectacular view of London. The sun was just starting to appear on the horizon.

Mackinnon swallowed hard as he thought the London skyline was probably the last thing Beverley Madison saw.

CHAPTER FOUR

I'D GONE STRAIGHT HOME LAST night after killing Beverley Madison, but I couldn't resist coming back the following morning. I needed to know what was going on.

The police had closed the street to traffic, and the blue and white police tape flickered in the cold December air.

I ducked my chin low and smiled beneath my grey wool scarf. There were so many people here.

Crowds of onlookers had gathered at the tape, desperate to find out what had happened, and I fitted in as just another nosy member of the public.

As I stepped closer to the hotel entrance, my pulse spiked. I had really done it! After all those years of planning...

When I'd woken up this morning, I'd been convinced it had all been a dream.

I overheard a couple of people beside me, gossiping about what had happened last night.

"It was a suicide," someone said.

"Nah, there's too many coppers for that," a young Asian man said.

"I heard it was an assassination... a diplomat," an older woman said, with a sparkle of excitement in her eyes.

And when the man beside her whispered, "Murder." I felt a thrill run through me and grinned again, although I was careful to keep my face hidden with my scarf. I'd worn a different coat today — dark red with no hood. I didn't want anything to link me to last night.

I knew the place had to be crammed full of security cameras, but that couldn't be helped. I'd avoided them as much as I could, but no one could escape them entirely. Eventually, the police would catch up with me. I could only hope they didn't close in on me before I was ready.

I still had plans.

I moved away from the crowd of gossips, drifting closer to the marked police cars, so I could watch the police work.

Behind me there was a kerfuffle and a loud voice was demanding people move aside. When I turned around, I saw a man I recognised from Sky News, followed by a TV crew. Wow. TV *already*. Good. Publicity was all part of the plan. Although, I hadn't expected it to come quite so quickly.

I turned back to the police. They were made up mostly of uniformed officers, but I saw two plain-clothed detectives, a man in a suit with grey hair and a tall well-built man next to him. It was obvious they were detectives. I would have guessed that even if the grey-haired one hadn't been ordering people around.

The tall detective turned away from his colleague and scanned the crowd. For a moment, he looked directly at me.

I fought the instinct to run as my heart slammed against my ribs.

Don't be ridiculous. He doesn't know it's you. He can't know.

I was jostled from behind by someone shouting and asking for a statement. A young man with a ponytail was holding a Dictaphone above his head and waving at the police officers. I took that as my cue to slip away, hiding behind the rest of the crowd that had already started to swell.

The ponytailed journalist didn't get his statement. But his disappointment didn't last long. He didn't let the police's silence hold him back from getting his story.

A woman just ahead of us was leaving the hotel, wheeling a Louis Vuitton overnight case behind her. The ponytailed journalist immediately switched his attention to her.

"Miss? Miss? Were you staying at the hotel? Can you tell me what happened?"

The woman pushed her dark hair out of her face and then pressed her hand against her chest as her face took on a pained expression. I immediately disliked her. She was obviously a dramatic type who enjoyed being the centre of attention.

"Oh," she said. "It was just terrible. A woman has been killed. She was only one floor above mine. Just awful. I've been questioned by the police. Of course, I had to check out today. I couldn't stay there another minute."

The press pack flooded towards her, shouting their questions.

"Please," she said. "I'm too upset. I just need a taxi, and the police have blocked off the road. I mean, what are the guests supposed to do? It's so inconvenient."

The ponytailed journalist lifted the crime scene tape for her. "Come with me. You've had such a terrible shock, but don't worry. I know where you can get a taxi. Here, let me take your case. Now, tell me what happened to the poor woman last night?"

As the journalist led her down the street, their voices faded, and I turned my attention back to the detectives heading for an unmarked car.

I had to wonder how much they knew already.

Not much, I thought. They wouldn't even have found the little clue I'd left for them yet.

CHAPTER FIVE

BACK AT WOOD STREET STATION, the site of the City of London police headquarters since 2002, DI Tyler took the morning briefing, as DCI Brookbank was preparing to give a statement to the press.

As the team filed into the largest meeting room at Wood Street, Mackinnon took the seat next to DC Charlotte Brown. She sipped her coffee then smiled at him. "This sounds like a particularly nasty one."

Mackinnon nodded. He couldn't get the image of Beverley Madison's bloated and misshapen body out of his head.

Once everyone had gathered together, DI Tyler stood beside the whiteboard. A blown-up head shot of Beverley Madison, which had been taken from her driver's license, had been tacked to the white surface.

Tyler nodded at the image as he began his introduction. "Beverley Madison, aged thirty-nine. Her body was discovered in her hotel room at six-thirty this morning. She had arranged an alarm call last night, as she was booked onto a flight from City airport this morning. When she didn't respond to the wake-up call or answer the door when room service delivered her breakfast, the hotel staff checked the room.

"Preliminary investigations have revealed no obvious cause of death, although as you can see from the crime scene photographs in your files her body was extremely swollen and bloated. It's *possible* an allergic reaction played a role, so any allergies Beverley had will be important to the investigation. Time of death would have been sometime after eleven pm, when she was last seen in the bar, and six-thirty am when her body was discovered by the hotel staff. We will get a more accurate time window after the post-mortem.

"Beverley wasn't married, or even in a relationship, as far as we know. Her only surviving family is a niece and an elderly father, who has advanced Alzheimer's, so it is unlikely the father will be able to help us. We have informed her niece as she is next of kin. Obviously she's distraught, but she's been able to talk to us and give us some details about her aunt's life. As far as she was aware, her aunt wasn't allergic to anything, but she hadn't actually seen Beverley in almost two years. She said there was no falling out. The lack of contact was just because they lived such busy lives."

DC Webb said, "Beverley Madison was a wealthy woman. Does the niece inherit?"

"We don't know yet. We've got the name of Beverley's solicitor, Dubbs and Drakes. So we'll look into it.

"It's not looking like a sex crime, and we know it wasn't a robbery. She was wearing a valuable gold and sapphire ring and a diamond bracelet was out in full view, yet it wasn't touched."

DC Collins huffed out a breath and set down his file on the table. "I've never seen anything like it. What could have caused her body to swell up like that?"

"Hopefully the post-mortem will give us something to go on. CSU are still combing the hotel suite." Tyler tapped his pen on the desk. "We need to find out what she was doing in the twenty-four hours before her death. I want to know where she went, who she saw, what she ate and drank. I want to know everything. I want a complete picture of Beverley's life. No detail is too small.

"DC Hassan is going to be coordinating the search team at her flat in St John's Wood. DC Collins, I need you to coordinate the canvassing of the hotel staff and guests. I've set it up this morning, but I want you to take over the management, okay?"

Collins nodded unenthusiastically.

"How did you get on with the CCTV?"

Collins looked down at his file and flipped it open. "Promising. There are cameras in the lifts, and in the corridors. There are problems, though. The cameras in the bar were facing towards the staff behind the bar rather than the customers. We know Beverley was in the bar, but we can't see who she met or talked to while she was there. Also, the hotel has been having a problem with the motion sensing lights on the forty-fourth floor, which means the CCTV footage from the corridor leading to Beverley Madison's room isn't great quality. It's producing very dark images, mainly shadows, and it's not easy to interpret."

Tyler frowned.

"We should still be able to identify anyone travelling to that floor and through the lobby, so it isn't a total loss," Collins quickly added. "I've seen footage of Beverley Madison travelling in the elevator up to the forty-fourth floor at four minutes past eleven."

"Was she alone?"

"Yes."

"Can you see her going into her room?"

Collins shook his head. "The CCTV from the corridor is too dark and grainy to make it out, but we might be able to get it enhanced."

"Fine. Get it enhanced. Then we need to see who else travelled up to the forty-fourth floor in the elevator. Maybe someone followed her."

"Maybe the killer took the stairs," DC Webb suggested.

Collins shook his head. "The doors to the stairwells are alarmed, and they are only supposed to be used in case of fire. No alarms were triggered."

"It could be that whoever killed Beverley was already on the forty-fourth floor, waiting for her," Mackinnon said. "What about the service lifts?"

Collins nodded. "They are monitored too, but I haven't looked at any of the CCTV yet. Both sets of lifts require an activated key card. So for example, a guest can only select a floor if they insert their key card below the touch pad."

DI Tyler nodded at Charlotte. "You can take over from Collins on managing the footage from the CCTV. Let me know who you can identify from the lifts."

"Yes, boss."

"That will leave Collins free to oversee the canvassing of the hotel. Out of all of those people, staff and guests, someone must have heard or seen something last night."

DI Tyler turned to Mackinnon. "I want you to focus on her work, Jack. Talk to the staff at the agency she owned. Find out if she was worried about anything, and also ask about any allergies. It seems that, in the case of Beverley Madison, her work colleagues will probably know more about her than her family does."

DI Tyler grabbed up the file from his desk and tucked it under his arm. "Any questions?"

There were a few murmurs around the room, but no questions. "Okay," DI Tyler said. "Get to work."

As they filed out of the meeting room and headed outside, Mackinnon was leafing through the pages of the file Tyler had given him, looking for the address of the Madison agency that Beverley Madison had owned. He located it on page four.

"Hey, take a look at this." Charlotte handed Mackinnon her phone as they walked across to their desks. She had the Twitter app open on Beverley Madison's account. Her last tweet had been sent at nine pm last night.

Fantastic day at the book fair! Time to celebrate with champagne!

Just two hours later, Beverley Madison had returned to her hotel room never to leave it again.

Mackinnon swiped his thumb across the screen and scrolled back a few tweets.

Are you thick? No unsolicited manuscripts.

Mackinnon raised an eyebrow. "Ouch, not exactly out to win friends on Twitter, was she?"

"Scroll down further," Charlotte said.

Did you even bother to check my website?!! I don't rep kids fiction, you fool!

"She certainly didn't believe in letting people down gently," Charlotte said. "There's lots more of the same and one particularly angry exchange with a writer last week."

"We'd better make a copy of that, and get the tech team to look into the people behind these Twitter handles.

"She definitely had an abrasive personality."

Mackinnon nodded. "But surely a cruel tweet is not enough for a motive."

"We have seen people kill for less," Charlotte said sadly as she took back her phone.

CHAPTER SIX

I WAS ACTUALLY TREMBLING. I was so nervous. I hadn't even been this nervous when I'd taken my driver's test.

This was worse than a job interview.

I was sitting on a hardback plastic chair next to a woman with a shaved undercut, who was cradling a grizzling baby. Behind us there were two men in their forties who barely seemed able to keep awake, despite the noise coming from the baby.

The two women behind the counter were ignoring us and ignoring the phones ringing on their desks too.

Instead of working, they were chatting about the television show they'd watched last night, one of those stupid singing competitions. The older of the two women giggled as she sipped her coffee.

They were driving me crazy. This was what my taxes were paying for. No wonder this country was going to the dogs.

The man in the row of chairs behind me began tapping his foot.

Tap…tap…tap.

I clenched my fists. I was starting to feel claustrophobic. It was so hot in here. The irritating peal of the telephone started up again and still they ignored it.

I stood up abruptly. "Are you going to answer that?"

The women behind the counter looked back at me with blank faces. After a pause the older woman said, "We are on a break."

I shook my head.

Unbelievable.

"Please sit down. Miss Carter will see you soon."

She stared hard at me until I reluctantly sat down. *The uppity, work-shy bitch.*

They went back to ignoring me. But finally they started to do some work, although they didn't get up from their seats. They kept their backsides firmly planted in their chairs, but propelled themselves on the wheels towards the filing cabinets.

I recalled an old proverb: *The sluggard will not plow by reason of the cold; Therefore shall he beg in harvest, and have nothing.*

I glanced at the clock. Twenty minutes past my appointment time. I was going to be late for work at this rate. It was beyond a joke. I was so tempted to get up and walk out of there, but I wouldn't.

I couldn't do it.

Goddamn social services.

I heard a door open along the corridor, and Gabby Carter stepped outside her office, all eighteen stone of her.

I stood up and walked towards her, not bothering to wait for those stupid women behind the counter to call my name. I ignored their beady stares as I walked passed them.

"Nice to see you again," Gabby said as she walked back inside her office.

I took a seat in front of her desk which was littered with brown foolscap files, other cases like mine, no doubt.

I wanted to talk. I had a whole speech worked out, and it had sounded so logical and convincing in my head, but now I was here in this poky office, the words abandoned me.

Gabby picked up a file from her desk and flicked through it briefly, then she dropped it back on her desk as if the contents bored her.

"Your mother's hands are healing well. That's good news, isn't it?" She spoke in a patronising voice, overly bright and cheerful.

She picked up a half-full cup of coffee and took a sip.

I stared in disgust at the half-eaten Mars bar on the side of her desk.

"She's settling in well at the care home," Gabby continued and shot a glance at the file. "Doris, one of the daycare staff, says your mum's very keen on the rhubarb crumble."

Gabby chuckled.

I bit down hard on the inside of my mouth. That was an outright lie. My mother hated sodding rhubarb.

"When can she come home?" I asked, deliberately not meeting Gabby's eyes. Instead, I focused on straightening the collar of my shirt.

I heard the chair creak, and I knew Gabby had shifted her position. But I didn't expect what she did next.

She reached out and patted my arm.

I flinched.

"We've spoken about this. Your mother isn't going to be able to stay at home. She requires full-time care now, and with your job…" Gabby shook her head.

"I have to work. What do you expect me to do? Quit my job? If I did, how would we afford to live?"

Gabby raised her palms. "I know, I know. I don't expect you to quit your job. It's too much to expect you to care for your mum and work full-time. That's why it's best for your mum to stay at Daffodil House. She gets around the clock care there, doesn't she? It really is the best thing for everyone."

I stared at Gabby, hating everything about her.

Best for whom? Not my mother. Not me.

She must be so confused. She was away from everything that was familiar to her and surrounded by strangers.

I tried again. "Why can't you let her stay with me? If you could arrange some assistance…perhaps a home help. That wouldn't be as expensive as full-time care and—"

"I'll have to stop you there," Gabby said. "She needs more than home help, and I think you know that. Her hands…well, you saw what happened. She scalded her hands. Next time, it could be worse."

I felt the tightness building in my chest. She was blaming me.

It was my fault my mother had burned her hands, my fault she'd poured boiling hot water all over them when she'd decided to have a boiled egg for lunch, and my fault she had sat there in pain all afternoon until I got home from work because she couldn't remember the number to call for an ambulance.

With my cheeks burning, I lowered my head.

"I am on your side," Gabby said. "I just want your mum to be safe."

I said nothing. I just stared at my hands resting in my lap. I wasn't seeing my hands, though. I saw the red, raw skin of my mother's hands after she'd scalded them.

"Well, that's sorted then," Gabby said, heaving herself to her feet. "I'm glad we've come to an understanding. I've got a ton of other appointments this morning." She tilted her head and gave me an embarrassed smile. "I know it's daft, but I had it in my head that you might cause a fuss, silly, eh?"

I stared at her coldly. Oh, I would make a fuss all right.

Gabby would realise soon enough that I wasn't a person to be messed with.

CHAPTER SEVEN

THE MADISON LITERARY AGENCY WAS on Orange Street, just around the corner from the National Portrait Gallery and next door to a Cafe Nero coffee shop.

Mackinnon showed his ID at the reception. Beverley's partner at the agency, Aaron Huxley, had been informed of Beverley's death, and Mackinnon guessed he must have already told the rest of the staff.

The female receptionist looked up at him through blood-shot eyes and dabbed her nose with a scrunched up tissue.

"You're here about Beverley," she said. "I can't believe it...none of us can. I suppose you want to speak to Alice first? Mr. Huxley said you would."

"Alice?"

"Alice Read. She was Beverley Madison's personal assistant."

Mackinnon nodded. "Yes, thank you. I would like to speak to her."

"I'll just give her a ring and let her know you're here."

Mackinnon thanked her and turned his attention to the small reception area, which was decorated solely in black and white. The only splashes of colour came from the blown-up book jackets, hanging in frames on the wall.

One particularly eye-catching cover had a machete, dripping with blood, on the cover. The author's name, Jacob Jansen, was written in blood-red bold type.

"Alice is ready to see you now. If you'd like to follow me?" The receptionist smiled weakly when she saw Mackinnon looking at the book cover.

"That's Jacob's latest," she said, with obvious pride.

"I heard he is one of the agency's top sellers," Mackinnon said.

"Oh, yes. *Sunday Times* number one on every release for the past five years. He's brilliant. I've met him a few times. He's ever so charming."

The receptionist led Mackinnon along a corridor until they reached a door with Beverley Madison's nameplate. "Alice is in here. She's trying to sort out Beverley's office."

Mackinnon frowned. "What?"

When the door opened, a small, dark-haired woman looked up from the desk. She stood up and then offered Mackinnon her hand. "Detective, my name is Alice Read."

Mackinnon stared angrily at the woman who had been rifling through Beverley Madison's desk. "Alice, I will have to ask you to leave Beverley Madison's office and possessions alone until we say otherwise. They are part of a murder inquiry."

"Oh, but…"

"You could be tampering with important evidence.

33

Weren't you informed that we would be sending out a crime scene unit?"

"Well, yes, but this isn't actually a crime scene, is it? I was only giving it a quick tidy and Mr. Huxley insisted." Alice Read shot a glance at the receptionist, who was still standing beside Mackinnon.

"You can leave us now. Thank you, Tara," she said pointedly.

"Aaron Huxley asked you to do this?"

Alice Read nodded. "Mr. Huxley is the junior partner in the agency. He wants to move offices…"

Mackinnon raised an eyebrow. "That's fast work."

Alice Read flushed. "Sorry, if it seems insensitive." She rubbed her forehead and looked down at the desk. "I just wanted to keep busy."

"Is there somewhere else we can talk?" Mackinnon asked.

Alice Read nodded. She locked Beverley Madison's office behind them and took Mackinnon to a small refreshment area a short distance away.

She gestured to the coffee machine, but when Mackinnon shook his head, she sat down at the table. Mackinnon sat opposite.

"I know it's not easy when someone you know well passes away, especially in circumstances like this, but I need to ask you some questions. Is that okay?"

Alice Read nodded. "Everyone has been saying Beverley was murdered. Was she really? Do you have any idea who did it?"

"We are still at a very early stage of the investigation,"

Mackinnon said. "Could you tell me if Beverley was romantically involved with anyone?"

"Not to my knowledge. In fact, she made a joke about it the other day. Said she had been single forever." Alice Read's eyes filled with tears.

"How long have you worked for her, Alice?"

"Seven years."

"Was she easy to work for?"

Alice Read smiled. "Oh, I wouldn't say that exactly. She was rather particular, but she had a good heart."

"Had she had any disagreements with anyone recently? Arguments?"

Alice shook her head, but she bit her lip at the same time.

"Are you sure?" Mackinnon pressed her. "It might not seem important to you now, but we need to find out as much as we can."

Alice Read hesitated. "Well…she did have a bit of a rant the other day. It was about one of her major clients, Jacob Jansen."

Mackinnon nodded. "Go on. What happened?"

"Well, that's just it. I don't know exactly what happened. All I know is that Beverley came into work last Wednesday in a foul mood. She was fuming. She said something about Jacob really going too far this time, and she said she wasn't going to let him get away with it."

"What had he done?"

"I really don't know. You see, they can all be a bit theatrical around here. I just thought it would all blow over so I didn't really pay much attention. They were always falling out."

"Jacob Jansen and Beverley?"

"Yes, they had a tempestuous relationship at the best of times, but well, I'm sure Jacob has nothing to do with what has happened to Beverley, Detective. I spoke to him this morning, and he is really distraught over what has happened. We all are."

Mackinnon nodded. They would have to take a close look at Jacob Jansen's relationship with Beverley Madison.

"Did Beverley talk much about her relatives?" Mackinnon asked.

"Well, I know her father is in a care home in Hampstead."

Mackinnon nodded.

"And she does have a niece," Alice continued. "I think she used to spend Christmas with her until they had a falling out."

"Do you know why they fell out?" Mackinnon asked.

Alice shook her head. "I'm afraid not."

"What about allergies? Do you know if Beverley was allergic to anything?"

Alice frowned. "Allergic? Well, she did suffer from hay fever."

"Anything more extreme?"

Alice shook her head again. "Not that I know of."

Mackinnon asked Alice a few more questions but didn't feel like he was getting very far. "Perhaps I could have a chat with Mr. Huxley," he suggested.

Alice nodded. "Of course."

They found Aaron Huxley bundling his possessions into boxes.

"Preparing for a move are we, sir?" Mackinnon asked.

Aaron looked up, his eyes widening slightly, and his gaze flickered to Alice and then back to Mackinnon. "I take it you're a police officer? Here about Beverley?"

"Detective Sergeant Mackinnon, City of London Police. I was hoping to have a quick word and ask you a few questions about Beverley."

"Of course," Aaron Huxley said as he sat back down in his chair and gestured for Mackinnon to take the seat in front of his desk.

Alice Read left them to it.

"What was Beverley like to work with?"

"Oh, she was fantastic," Aaron said. "An absolute genius. I was so fortunate to learn from one of the best in the business."

As he spoke he didn't meet Mackinnon's gaze. His words sounded rehearsed and insincere.

"I'd heard she could be difficult to get along with at times," Mackinnon said, wanting to be sensitive, but at the same time, wanting to get down to the truth.

Aaron looked uncomfortable. "Well, I know how people talk, but really there isn't any truth to the rumours." Aaron folded his arms across his chest.

Mackinnon leaned forward, smiling. "Really?"

"People just like to stir things up," Aaron said and scowled. "The thing is, they don't understand our relationship."

"What don't they understand?"

"Well," he said and licked his lips. "We're creative. Passionate. We believe in our clients and sometimes we don't exactly see eye-to-eye, but deep down, I've always had the greatest respect for Beverley, and she knew that."

"You argued?"

"I wouldn't say that exactly. At times, our vision for the company wasn't in complete alignment. Sometimes, we had differences of opinion."

Mackinnon nodded. "You had a disagreement, then?"

Aaron tutted and looked away, in the direction of the window. "It really wasn't *my* fault. I was perfectly reasonable about it. I just wanted to make Beverley see that Jacob was our best client, and we needed to keep him. You know, it really is just common sense. Seventy percent of the agency's earnings come through Jacob Jansen," Aaron Huxley said, poking his desk to emphasise his point. "Beverley was Jacob's agent, but recently he had taken to calling me because she didn't reply to his emails or calls. I tried to make her see sense. We simply couldn't afford to lose someone like Jacob Jansen."

Mackinnon stared at Aaron until he flushed and looked away.

"And what did Beverley say to that?"

Aaron's cheeks flushed even redder and he didn't answer at first.

"It's best if you're honest with me," Mackinnon said.

"She said, I was just a little boy trying to play adult games that I didn't understand," he mumbled, looking down at his hands.

After a moment, he looked up. His eyes were flashing with indignation. "She was wrong! I've learned a lot from Beverley, but in this case..." He shook his head. "In this case, she was most definitely wrong."

CHAPTER EIGHT

OVER THE NEXT TWO HOURS, Mackinnon spoke to everyone else at the Madison agency.

When he left, stepping outside onto Orange Street, he headed next door to Cafe Nero, pulling his mobile phone out of his pocket and dialling DI Tyler.

Tyler answered on the third ring. "Any luck? What did you get out of her colleagues?"

Mackinnon walked into the coffee shop and stood in line. He was surprised to see Aaron Huxley at the counter, buying a toasted sandwich.

Aaron noticed Mackinnon and nodded, giving him a small smile.

"I've got something that could be of interest to us," Mackinnon said, keeping his voice down. "I'm just in a cafe, picking up a coffee and then I'll come straight back to the station. Any news on your end?"

"Couple of things on the CCTV," Tyler said. "It's given

us something to go on. Obviously, not a lovely clear face shot. That would be *too* easy." Tyler sighed. "Collins is still working his way through the hotel guests with the team. That's taking him a while. Brookbank has spoken to the press this morning. We're keeping it as low-key as we can. And I'm about to head off to the post-mortem, so if you've managed to get a great lead, you'd better tell me about it now."

A few feet ahead of Mackinnon, Aaron Huxley picked up his toasted sandwich and carried it past Mackinnon towards the exit.

Now that Aaron Huxley was out of earshot, Mackinnon filled Tyler in. "Beverley had no allergies except hay fever, according to her PA, but as we have already gathered, Beverley Madison was known to have a somewhat abrasive personality. There was an incident last Wednesday when she was overheard ranting about a client, a writer by the name of Jacob Jansen."

Mackinnon covered the mouthpiece of the phone and asked the barista for an Americano.

"Jacob Jansen? The thriller writer? Even *I* have heard of *him*," Tyler said.

"Apparently, Beverley had been his agent for years, but they haven't been getting on well lately, and at one point last week, Beverley was overheard by her PA saying that Jacob Jansen had gone too far this time."

"Interesting." Tyler paused as if he was mulling things over. "I want you to go and talk to this Jacob Jansen. Right now. Until our questioning at the hotel produces some information, we've not got much to go on. I'd like to know exactly what this Jacob Jansen character did to push Beverley Madison too far."

Mackinnon paid for his coffee and carried it outside.

"I've got the address," Mackinnon said. "It's in Hampshire."

"Take one of the pool cars," Tyler said. "I won't be here when you get back. I've got to attend the post-mortem in a minute." Tyler exhaled deeply on the other end of the phone. "I'm not looking forward to it. That's for sure. Did you uncover anything else?"

"Not much," Mackinnon admitted. "She was a prickly character and had a few disagreements with Aaron Huxley, the junior partner, but the only one she had a real big blow up with recently was Jacob Jansen."

"All right," DI Tyler said. "Go and have a word with him and let me know how you get on."

CHAPTER NINE

DI TYLER HATED GOING TO post-mortems at the best of times, but he was really dreading this one.

By rights, it should have been Brookbank attending, but Brookbank wasn't any more keen than Tyler and so he'd delegated.

Just his luck, Tyler thought as he pushed open the door. The PM was being carried out by Dr. Edward Green, the most pompous man Tyler had ever had the pleasure of working with.

Just because he knew it would annoy Dr. Green, Tyler treated him to a broad grin. "What's up, Doc?"

The doctor gave Tyler a cold appraising look and replied with a single nod. He was already gowned up and ready to make a start. On the stainless steel table in front of him was the bloated body of Beverley Madison.

"You're late," Dr. Greene commented. "I'm just about to get started."

Tyler shrugged. He wasn't bothered. He wanted answers, but he didn't really want to watch the doctor carve through Beverley Madison's body in order to get them.

Dr. Green peered down his nose disapprovingly at Tyler.

"Kits hanging up," the doctor said, nodding to the pegs on the wall by the door.

Tyler took a light green cover-up from the peg and selected a clean mask. He put on the silly green hat last. He hated them. He didn't bother tying the mask at the back of his head, but instead, just held it against his mouth. He walked across to the doctor, but kept himself at least a foot away from the body.

"What have we got?" Tyler asked.

"The toxicology screen indicated a high level of alcohol in her blood, but there are other signs to make me think that she would be tolerant to that level of alcohol."

"Do we have a time of death yet, Doc?" Tyler asked. He kept calling him Doc purely because he knew it annoyed him.

Dr. Green frowned and then a small smile played over his lips. "Well," he said, "why don't you take a closer look here? I think you might find it interesting."

Tyler hesitated then leaned in close to the body. The smell of the mortuary made his stomach churn. Some officers put Vicks vapour rub beneath their noses to try and mask the smell, but to Tyler it only seemed to make it worse so he used nothing.

Beverley Madison's body looked even more bloated and bruised than it had done at the hotel when he'd first seen her body.

Tyler felt a bubbling sensation in his stomach and

wished he hadn't eaten that bacon butty earlier this morning. He leaned against the cold, stainless steel bench.

"So what am I looking for exactly?" He had his suspicions that Dr. Greene was enjoying his discomfort.

But Tyler wasn't green. Post-mortems were a necessary part of the job, and as much as he didn't like it, he knew it was necessary. He wasn't about to run out of the room and throw up like some kind of newbie.

Dr. Green placed his latex glove covered hands on the deceased's head and left shoulder and pried apart the bloated folds of flesh on her neck.

"Just here," Dr. Green said. "Can you see it?"

Tyler couldn't really see much of anything apart from a blotchy area of skin, but most of the rest of her was blotchy anyway.

He leaned over and looked a little closer, and then he saw it.

A tiny speck of blood at the centre of a localised bruise.

Tyler looked up at Dr. Green, feeling a rush of excitement. "Injection mark?"

Dr. Green stared at Tyler. "The cause of death is an odd one," he said. "Snake venom."

Tyler straightened up. "Snake venom," he repeated.

The doctor nodded slowly.

Tyler let out a low whistle. "Well, I didn't see that one coming. Any idea what type of snake?" he said leaning over again to peer at the mark on Beverley Madison's neck.

"Not yet," Dr. Green said. "But I'm hopeful we will have some answers soon. We are running tests, which should give us a clue, at least help us identify the species."

Tyler nodded, and then looked up at the doctor with a

grin. "I can only see one puncture wound in her neck. Are you telling me we've got a one-fanged snake slithering its way around London?"

Tyler smiled widely at his own joke, but the doctor didn't.

Dr. Green replied, deadpan, "That puncture wound is from a hypodermic syringe."

"So someone injected her with snake venom, and it caused her to bloat up like this."

The doctor tilted his head to one side. "It did. It's not the reaction you might expect. I'll be very interested in the type of snake they used."

"So will I," Tyler said. "It will give us something to go on."

Tyler stood by, feeling sick, as the doctor examined the stomach contents. He tried to keep his breathing shallow as the doctor got to work on Beverley Madison's body. This was easily the worst part of the job.

Finally when the doctor had almost finished, Tyler started to walk away. "If that's it then, Doc, I'll leave you to finish up."

Near the door, Tyler shrugged off the green coverall and stuffed it in the basket beside the stainless steel bench. The smell was really getting to him now, and he couldn't wait to get out of there. "I'll expect your report later today?"

"My *preliminary* report," Dr. Green said. "Yes, although it will take longer to identify the species of snake."

"Fine," Tyler said, tearing off the silly green hat and shoving it in the same basket as the coverall.

"Thanks, Doc," Tyler said cheerfully and pushed open the door. He breathed in the semi-fresh air as he left the mortuary. That had to rank as one of the worst post-mortems he had ever attended. They were always unpleas-ant. When the body was distorted like Beverley Madison's, it was pretty horrific. But the worst ones were the children. They were the ones that left him wanting a stiff drink immediately afterwards.

CHAPTER TEN

DC COLLINS GAVE A WEARY sigh and looked at his empty coffee cup. He picked it up and headed out into the lobby area of the hotel to ask for a refill. Coffee was just about the only thing keeping him going right now. Coordinating the canvassing of a hotel this size wasn't easy. Thankfully, the team had been allocated a number of uniforms to help with the questioning. But in a hotel where guests were constantly coming in and going out, it wasn't easy to keep track of everyone.

Collins smiled as one of the hotel staff came up and held out her hand for his empty coffee cup.

"I'll get you another," she said, anticipating his request, before he'd even opened his mouth.

The staff at the hotel had been brilliant. Considering how awful this must be for them and how worried they had to be about the murder hurting the hotel's reputation,

Collins had been expecting some resistance, but so far they'd done everything they could to help.

His phone beeped with an incoming email from Charlotte. Collins quickly skimmed the contents and then focused on the images attached to the message.

He sat down on one of the comfortable, well-cushioned chairs in the lobby, staring at the first CCTV image on his phone.

Most of the guests and staff travelling up to the forty-fourth floor had been identified and traced. The team were now in the process of interviewing and eliminating people from their list of potential suspects. However, Charlotte had sent a still from the CCTV, showing an unidentified hooded figure travelling in the elevator only fifteen minutes after Beverley Madison had retired to her room. It fitted the window of opportunity. Was this Beverley Madison's killer?

Collins scanned the text of the email again. According to Charlotte, the person had got out on the forty-fourth floor and headed in the direction of Beverley Madison's room. Although they didn't have a close-up image of the suspect's face, Collins couldn't help feeling hopeful.

Due to the dark corridors, the CCTV outside Beverley Madison's room was worse than useless, but they still had a chance to identify this unknown person.

The hooded figure had not been alone in the elevator.

Collins studied the image. There was a man, with a mobile phone clamped to his ear, standing next to the hooded figure. What were the chances the man on the phone would be able to identify this potential suspect?

He scrolled down to another still image from the CCTV. The man was looking directly at their unknown subject.

Charlotte had written that they had exchanged words in the elevator. There was no sound on the recording from the CCTV, but even so, Collins felt a rush of excitement. If they could identify this man, they might be able to get a description of their suspect.

The young Asian woman returned with Collins' coffee and set it down on the low glass table in front of him. Collins smiled, thanked her and then dialled Charlotte's number.

"We need to identify the other passenger in the lift," Collins said, without preamble.

"Agreed. You might have already questioned him. He had a key card, which operated the lift. So we think he is a guest on the same floor as Beverley Madison. From the CCTV, we can see him put his key card in and select the forty-fourth floor. The person in the navy hooded coat doesn't use a key, but exits the elevator at the same floor as our mystery man and heads straight to Beverley Madison's room.

"We've got the same person, wearing the navy coat, travelling back down in the elevator just ten minutes later. Then at the exit, leaving the hotel."

"So we don't think that the guy in the hooded coat was a guest at the hotel? Did he use a key card to travel down in the lift?"

"No, but you only need a key card if you want to access guest floors. The elevator will travel to the lobby and bar areas without guest keys.

"We're looking back through the rest of the footage now to see if we can identify him coming into the hotel itself. We need a shot of his face."

"It's possible that they are working together." Collins said.

"I don't think so," Charlotte said. "They don't look at each other until they are in the lift and the contact between them is brief."

"But if they were aware of the cameras that might be how they wanted it to look."

"True. I guess we can't rule it out."

Collins reached out for his coffee and took a sip. "Okay, I should have more luck identifying the second passenger. At least we can see his face. Keep me in the loop."

"Will do."

After Collins hung up, he drained the steaming cup of coffee and headed for the bar area.

The bar wasn't open yet, but there were some hotel staff milling about, putting lunch menus on tables, setting out chairs and polishing the bar.

Collins walked straight up to the bar and introduced himself. "I'd like to speak to whoever was in charge of the bar last night at around eleven pm."

The man behind the bar ran a hand through his spiky hair and nodded. "I was working last night, managing the bar. You're asking questions about the woman who was killed, aren't you?"

Collins nodded.

"I saw her." He had a pained expression. "I still can't believe it."

"What's your name, please, sir?" Collins asked.

"Lennie," the barman said. "Lennie Newton. I've already spoken to the police officers. I told them I saw her briefly last night. She came in for about forty minutes."

Collins nodded and made a mental note to go over Lennie Newton's statement as soon as he finished here. Collins took a look around the bar and took in the stunning view over London. There were a huge number of tables and chairs in the bar, and Collins guessed the capacity would be over one hundred.

"It's a big place. You must have had lots of customers last night," Collins said. "Why did you remember Beverley Madison in particular?"

Lennie shrugged. "I'm good with faces, I suppose, and she ordered one of the most expensive champagnes on the menu. I did tell her the price. I know that most of the people that come here have quite enough money to buy it without a second thought. But it always shocks me that people are prepared to pay that much for a drink." Lennie shrugged. "So I remembered her. She laughed when I told her the price. Said her friend was paying."

Collins nodded. "Did she say anything else to you?"

"She just joked that her friend would put it on his expense account." Lennie shrugged again. "I don't know if she was serious. She seemed nice enough. Between you and me, I think she'd had quite a bit to drink before she got here."

Collins nodded. "What about the friend she was with?"

"Uh, yes. She was with an American gentleman. They came in together, but left separately, I think. I don't remember her leaving, but I do remember him paying the bill. It was just after eleven, I think."

"If he paid for the expensive Champagne, would you be able to locate the bill and perhaps tell me his name and his room number if he was a guest here?"

Lennie nodded. "Sure. It will just take a moment. You can take a seat if you want."

Collins walked away from the bar and sat on one of the chairs close to the window. He gazed out at the stunning skyline. It was surprising anyone had noticed anything last night with a view like that to look at. He opened up his email app and again studied the still from the CCTV. He didn't want to get his hopes up.

"Here we go," Lenny said cheerfully, coming towards Collins with a slip of paper.

"This was his bill. See there." Lennie pointed to the bill. "He paid for the champagne."

The figure on the bill made Collins' eyes water. After wincing at the exorbitant cost, he focused on the name at the bottom of the receipt.

Barry Henderson.

Room 4423.

Collins stood up. "Thank you very much. You've been a great help."

Lenny smiled. "Pleased to help."

Collins held out his phone with the image of the CCTV still on the screen. "Is this the man you saw last night with Beverley Madison?"

Lennie nodded. "Yeah, that's him. Definitely."

CHAPTER ELEVEN

COLLINS HEADED BACK TO THE incident room, just off the lobby area. The hotel had given them the use of one of the meeting rooms in the business centre to use as the control centre for the investigation.

The team had all their equipment and computers set up in there. Collins smiled at PC Mary Dowd as he walked in.

"I'm going up to see a Mr. Barry Henderson," Collins said. "I think he's on our list. Has he been interviewed yet?"

Mary tapped a couple of keys on her keyboard and stared at the computer screen. "Not yet. He's on the list, but he wasn't in his room when the uniforms called the first time. I believe he is still in the hotel though, sir. We don't have a record of him leaving today."

Collins nodded. "Good. I'll see if he's in his room now."

Collins stepped into the elevator and used the key card he'd been given by the hotel. The elevator swept him up to the forty-fourth floor in seconds.

When Collins stepped out, he couldn't help hoping that Barry Henderson would be able to tell them something that would take the case in a new direction. They needed to move as quickly as possible. The twenty-four hours following a murder were the most crucial in generating leads. It was when people's memories were freshest.

Collins knocked on Barry Henderson's door.

When ten seconds passed with no response, Collins raised his hand to knock again.

Bloody hell. The bloke better not have done a runner. Right now, he was their best chance of identifying their main suspect.

But before Collins could knock again, the door was opened and Barry Henderson looked at him in a sad, resigned way.

"Police, I presume," he said.

Collins showed his warrant card and introduced himself. "I'd like to ask you a few questions, Mr. Henderson."

"If you like," Henderson said with a shrug and stood back to allow Collins to enter the room.

It was a luxurious suite. The bed hadn't been made and the sheets were rumpled, but other than that, the rest of the room was tidy.

Barry Henderson sighed. "It's a horrible business," he said. "Poor Beverley."

"Did you know Beverley well?"

"Yes. I've known her for over twenty years. We both started off in the publishing business together. She worked in America for a time. Did you know that?"

Collins scribbled down a note. "When was that?"

"Oh, years ago. Back in the early nineties."

"Do you know of anyone who might have wanted to harm Beverley?"

Barry Henderson sighed again and looked up at the ceiling. "Well, she certainly wasn't Little Miss Popular. But I can't imagine anyone she knew would want to do this. She could be hard, detective, but you need to be in this business. She had to be ruthless sometimes in the best interest of her clients."

"Could you tell me where you were last night and what you were doing between ten pm and midnight?"

Barry Henderson blinked. "Why?"

"It's a question we are asking everybody, Mr. Henderson. We need to know people's whereabouts. It helps us work out a clear picture of events."

Barry Henderson shrugged. "I see. Well, I was at a launch party for a book, some ridiculous celebrity cookery book that they hadn't even written themselves. Of course it was written by a ghostwriter, which is so popular these days." Barry Henderson looked longingly at a packet of cigarettes on the dressing table. "After that, around eleven or so, I came back here with Beverley and we had a nightcap in the bar. She left before I did, but I didn't stay much longer. It had been a long day."

Collins asked a few more questions before pulling out his phone and showing the still image from the CCTV to Barry Henderson.

"Is this you, sir?"

Barry Henderson looked surprised. "Well, yes, it is. That's me last night."

"And who is that standing beside you?"

Barry Henderson blinked and looked back at the image. "I don't know. I don't even remember anyone else being in the elevator." Barry Henderson shrugged. "I don't have a clue who it is."

An understanding seemed to pass over Barry Henderson. A shadow flashed across his face. He raised a hand to his mouth. "Do you think that's the person who harmed Beverley?"

"We are just gathering the facts at the moment, sir," Collins said. "Now, you were on the phone at the time. Who were you speaking to?"

"My office, back in New York. I was just filling them in on the day. It was just business."

Collins nodded. He then zoomed in on the image of the hooded figure on his phone. "Just after you entered the elevator, you spoke to the person next to you. Do you remember what was said?"

Barry Henderson frowned as he tried to remember. "I don't recall. I don't think it was anything important... I think I probably just asked what floor they wanted."

"Okay," Collins said. "This individual exited the lift on the same floor as you."

Barry Henderson's face was creased with concern. "What are you saying, detective?"

"Did you notice if they had a hotel key card? Perhaps they mentioned wanting the forty-fourth floor."

Barry Henderson shook his head. "I don't remember. I don't think so."

"You put your key card into the panel and selected the forty-fourth floor," Collins said. "Were they holding their own key card?"

"No," Barry Henderson whispered, his face a mask of grave concern. He shuddered. "Detective, are you saying that I allowed the killer access to Beverley's floor? Was it my fault?"

"I'm not saying anything of the sort. This person hasn't been identified yet, and we need to make sure we know who they were and what they were doing here."

Barry Henderson didn't look convinced. He rubbed a weary hand over his face. "Oh, Christ. I can't believe this is happening."

"We are nearly finished now, sir," Collins said. "I just need you to give me a description of the person in the elevator."

"A description?" Barry Henderson repeated. "I really didn't pay very much attention."

"Well, we can see from the CCTV that they were wearing dark trousers, probably black and a navy blue hooded coat." Collins smiled encouragingly. "Any small detail you can remember could help us. Was it a man or woman?" Collins asked.

"Oh…" Barry Henderson said, and his forehead crinkled as he thought about it. "A man, I think," he said, slowly. "Young-looking. I mean…it could have been a woman, I suppose."

Collins felt disappointment flood through him. All his hopes of a good description of their main suspect were slowly trickling away. How could Barry Henderson not know whether the person he shared the elevator with, the person he *spoke* to, was male or female?

"What was their voice like? You spoke to them, didn't you?"

"Oh, yes," he said. "Well, it was low, I think, but not very deep." Barry Henderson put his head in his hands. "I'm so sorry. I don't know. I really can't remember…"

They were getting nowhere fast. Collins finished up with a few more questions and then asked Barry Henderson to keep the team aware of his movements as they may need to speak to him again.

As Collins left Barry Henderson's room, he reached for his mobile phone. He was going to have to give the bad news to DI Tyler, and he wasn't looking forward to it at all.

CHAPTER TWELVE

MACKINNON PULLED INTO THE LAY-by opposite Yateley Lodge in Hampshire. It had taken him just over an hour and a half. He couldn't see the house from where he was parked, but on the opposite side of the road there was a pair of majestic looking gates.

Beside the gates, there was a group of four men loitering. Two of the men carried cameras, and one of them looked over at Mackinnon's car with interest. Mackinnon guessed they were members of the press, hanging around, waiting for a statement from the famous writer Jacob Jansen after the death of his agent.

Before approaching the entrance, Mackinnon decided to ring DI Tyler. Tyler gave him a quick update and went over the questions he wanted Mackinnon to ask Jacob Jansen. After Mackinnon hung up the phone, he took a moment to think things through.

Snake venom was an unusual choice for a murder weapon. There were certainly easier ways to kill someone.

The whole case had a dash of the dramatic about it. Perhaps something a thriller writer might be interested in?

Mackinnon glanced ahead in the direction of the journalists hovering at the entrance.

He drove out of the lay-by and pulled up in front of the gates. The group of men slowly moved out of the way.

One of them rapped on the car window. "Police?" the man shouted with a grin on his face. "Any chance of a statement from you? Is Jacob Jansen a suspect?"

Mackinnon opened the car door, narrowly missing hitting the journalist on the hip.

As Mackinnon got out of the driver's seat, the man took a couple of steps backwards. Now looking a little less sure of himself, he blinked up at Mackinnon.

"We aren't doing anything wrong." The journalist looked round at the other men standing behind him. He folded his arms across his chest.

"No statement," Mackinnon said. "This is private property, and I'm sure Mr. Jansen wouldn't appreciate your presence here at this time."

"I wouldn't be so sure of that. Jacob has always been a friend to the press. He likes the publicity. You have come here to ask him about Beverley Madison, haven't you?"

"No comment." Mackinnon strode towards the gatepost and pressed the intercom.

Before Mackinnon could even introduce himself, a voice crackled, "He is on his way down. He won't keep you a moment."

Mackinnon frowned. He hadn't even said who he was or what he wanted.

Mackinnon walked back from the gates and leaned against the bonnet of the car.

"Do you think it was one of her clients?" The question came from one of the journalists. He had slicked back hair and was wearing a long brown coat. "Or was it a random killing?"

Mackinnon couldn't help smiling. "You don't give up easily, do you?"

The man smiled. "You don't get far in my game if you do."

"Sorry to keep you waiting," a loud voice boomed from behind the gates.

Mackinnon turned around and saw Jacob Jansen. He recognised him from the photographs at the literary agency. He was wearing a navy blue Barbour jacket, dark denim jeans and a pair of green Hunter Wellington boots.

A pair of black Labradors stood by his heels. Jacob Jansen, who clearly enjoyed playing the country gentleman, smiled broadly at no one in particular and stuck his thumbs in his pockets.

"Now," he said, clearing his throat and pulling out a scrap of paper from his Barbour jacket. "I have a statement for you."

But before he could speak, he was interrupted by one of the journalists. "We've had reports that Beverley was killed with some kind of snake venom. Can you comment on that?"

Mackinnon whirled around. He had only just received

that information from Tyler a few moments ago. How could the press possibly have got hold of it?

"It's a terrible shock."

Mackinnon studied Jacob Jansen's reaction carefully.

He pressed a hand to his chest as if that would convey how deeply he was hurt. "I have worked with Beverley Madison for many years, and she was everything a writer could want in an agent. I am completely distraught at the news of her death, but I couldn't possibly comment on the involvement of snake venom. I'm afraid no one had mentioned that fact to me."

One of the men held up his camera taking multiple shots of Jacob Jansen.

"Stop that," Jacob Jansen said irritably. "I don't want you publishing a load of photographs with my mouth half open. You'll get a chance to take your photos at the end."

"Do you think she might have been the victim of a deranged serial killer?" The journalist with the slicked back hair held up his tape recorder as close to the gates and Jacob Jansen as he could.

"In my opinion," Jacob Jansen began, "it's highly likely we have an organised and very dangerous killer. I believe it's possible he will strike again." A thin smile spread on Jacob Jansen's lips. "In fact, I've just thought of a moniker you guys might like to use. You could call him…" Jacob Jansen paused for dramatic effect. "The Charmer."

Jacob Jansen spread his hands theatrically. "Yes," he said, nodding and looking incredibly pleased with himself. "The *Snake Charmer*."

Mackinnon had heard enough. He held up his warrant

card. "Detective Sergeant Mackinnon, City of London police. I'd like a word with you, Mr. Jansen."

The colour drained from Jacob Jansen's face. "Oh, goodness. I thought you were…"

"I know what you thought, sir. Now why don't you open the gate and we can have a chat."

"Oh, yes, of course," Jacob said. "Is that your car?"

Mackinnon nodded.

"Ah, good. Would you mind giving me a lift back up to the house. The boys, too," he said, nodding at the two black Labradors.

Mackinnon agreed and Jacob Jansen opened the gates.

"What about our photographs?"

Jacob Jansen waved his hand in dismissal at the four journalists. "Later."

Mackinnon drove the author and his Labradors along the winding driveway.

The house was huge. The small sign by the front door grandly named it Yateley Lodge.

Clearly, a career as a thriller writer had paid very well for Jansen.

Jansen opened the back door of the car, releasing the dogs, and they scrambled out and started chasing each other around the front lawns.

"Well, let's get inside out of the cold, shall we?" Jacob Jansen suggested with a hesitant smile. "Would you like a drink?"

"Coffee would be good, thanks," Mackinnon replied.

The inside of Yateley Lodge was no less impressive than the outside. The hardwood floors were polished to a gleaming shine, and a huge crystal chandelier hung over the entrance hall.

"This way," Jacob Jansen said, leading Mackinnon along the hallway into a huge country-style kitchen.

Jacob shrugged off his Barbour jacket and flung it across a chair. He moved across the kitchen to a coffee maker, which wouldn't have looked out of place in a coffee shop. The machine was a mass of gleaming metal.

As Jacob busied himself making the coffee, Mackinnon perched on a stool next to the central island in the kitchen.

"I guess you're here about Beverley," Jacob Jansen said, speaking loudly to be heard over the coffee bean grinder.

"That's right," Mackinnon said. "We're talking to people who knew her. We are especially interested in people who saw her recently. I wonder if you could tell me when you last saw Beverley Madison?"

Jacob Jansen leaned back against the kitchen counter. "Not that long ago," he said. "Actually, she popped by last week."

There was something in the way he moved, the tension in his shoulders. Even if Beverley Madison's PA hadn't tipped Mackinnon off, Jacob Jansen's body language alone would have been enough for Mackinnon to believe he was hiding something.

"What did she come down here for? Social call? Work?"

"Bit of both really. I think she was just checking up on me. I'm her major client, you know. I bring in a great deal of money for Beverley's agency."

Mackinnon nodded. "When she visited you, what kind of mood was she in?"

"Mood?" Jacob Jansen set two cups of coffee down on

the island and pushed one towards Mackinnon. "I can't say I noticed her mood."

"You can't remember if she was happy? Sad? Angry?"

Jacob Jansen looked down at his coffee cup. "She wasn't in any particular mood," he said eventually.

"I spoke to her personal assistant this morning, Alice Read. Do you know her?"

Jacob Jansen's mouth set in a thin line. He nodded. "Yes, I know Alice."

"Well, Alice told me something very interesting. She told me Beverley Madison was quite angry just before she came to see you. In fact, Alice told me Beverley said that you had pushed her too far this time. Can you tell me what she meant by that?"

Jacob Jansen raised his eyes from his coffee cup and glared at Mackinnon. "Oh, all right. Fine. Yes, she did come down here, and she was absolutely furious. She pulled up at the gates, didn't bother waiting for me to answer the intercom and let her in before yelling at me. She was screeching. I mean, it's lucky I don't have any neighbours close by."

Jacob shook his head. "I let her in, against my better judgement, and she started ranting and raving at me like a mad woman."

"You have been having a difficult relationship with your agent for some time, is that correct, Mr. Jansen?"

Jacob Jansen rolled his eyes. "It's hardly a secret. Her bloody agency takes fifteen percent of everything I earn, and yet I found out the other day she had a prime opportunity to sell the rights for two of my books to Japan, and she hadn't even bothered to contact them. They told me they've been trying to get in touch for ages to arrange a deal." Jacob Jansen shook his head. "She was taking advantage of me. She'd taken on too many new clients, spread herself too thin. And *I* was the one earning all the money, but they weren't giving *me* any attention."

"Why was Beverley Madison so angry when she came to see you? Something must have happened to get her so worked up."

Jacob Jansen got to his feet and walked over to a kitchen unit. He pulled open a drawer and fumbled around in it for a moment.

"It's ridiculous actually. As soon as I let her in the house, she threw this in my face."

He handed Mackinnon a scrap of paper that looked like it had been torn out of a newspaper. Beverley Madison's name was at the top,

When Mackinnon read the rest of the printed words, he felt his chest tighten.

It was an obituary.

"Did you send this to her?"

"Of course, I didn't. I told Beverley so. I said she was being ridiculous, but she wouldn't listen."

"So who would have sent this to her?"

"Take your pick," Jacob Jansen said. "She wasn't exactly flavour of the month with a lot of people. I know many of her other clients felt the same as I did, and she could be particularly cruel to aspiring writers. I think somebody probably sent it as a joke, trying to give her a scare, and it worked. You don't think..." Jacob Jansen frowned and looked up at Mackinnon. "You don't think it had anything to do with why she died?"

"I'll take this back to the station, if you don't mind, Mr. Jansen," Mackinnon said.

Jacob Jansen shrugged. "Be my guest. I don't want to keep the bloody thing."

Jacob took a sip of his coffee, then sighed. "You know, despite our differences, she did help me a great deal at the start of my career. It's horrible to think someone murdered her. What an awful way to die."

Mackinnon nodded. He wouldn't wish the gruesome death Beverley Madison had suffered on anyone.

CHAPTER THIRTEEN

I THOUGHT I HAD THE office to myself. It was after five pm, and everyone should have gone home. I sat in my cubicle and pulled out the newspaper from my bag.

I smiled as my gaze focused on the obituary.

Perfect.

I pulled a pair of scissors out of the drawer under my desk and used them to start cutting the edges of the obituary. It was the size of a business card and pleasantly understated.

I'd almost finished cutting it out when I felt a hand on my shoulder.

I jumped, catching the edge of my palm with the sharp point of the scissors.

I bundled my bag on top of the obituary page, trying to hide the evidence and then examined my palm. Luckily, the scissors hadn't punctured my skin.

"Sorry. Didn't mean to make you jump."

It was Sue, the woman who worked in the cubicle opposite me.

I forced myself to smile. "That's all right. I just thought everyone else had already gone home."

"Just on my way out," Sue said. "I came back for this." She held up a blue and yellow knitted scarf.

When I didn't reply, she looped the scarf around her neck. "Well, goodnight then."

She made as if she was going to walk away from me, then suddenly turned. "I couldn't help noticing...I hope you don't mind me asking, but you were looking at the obituary page. It wasn't anyone close to you, was it?"

Blood rushed to my cheeks. I shook my head.

"Only, I know you've had a rotten time of it just lately, what with your mother and everything."

I didn't want to talk about it. And I certainly didn't want to talk about it with Sue. I shoved the scissors back in the drawer and folded up the paper.

"If you ever need to talk to someone," Sue said and then shrugged. "Well, I'm here if you need me. In fact, a few of us are meeting up at The Three Bells if you want to join us? Brandy and Josh will be there."

I shook my head. "Thanks, but I can't tonight. I've got things to do."

Sue nodded as though she'd expected that answer. "Maybe another time. How is your mum doing? Is she getting on okay at that new place now?"

My fingers curled into fists, so that my fingernails dug into the flesh of my palms.

Of course she wasn't okay. What a stupid question.

"She is as well as can be expected," I said bluntly,

scooping up my bag and grabbing my laptop case. "I'll see you tomorrow. I have to get on. Like I said, I have things to do tonight."

It wasn't a lie. With what I had planned, I was going to have a very busy evening indeed.

CHAPTER FOURTEEN

DARKNESS HAD FALLEN BY THE time Mackinnon left Yateley Lodge and drove back along the M3 motorway towards London. It started to rain and the spray from the cars around him made it a miserable journey.

On the passenger seat next to him, contained in a plastic evidence bag, was the obituary he had taken from Jacob Jansen. Mackinnon's gaze flickered down to the torn scrap of paper before he turned his attention back to the road. Was it some kind of sick joke?

A fake obituary turning up days before Beverley Madison had been murdered was unlikely to be a coincidence.

Were they dealing with a sick killer who posted advance warnings to his victims?

He had called DI Tyler before he left Yateley Lodge, updating him on what he discovered from Jacob Jansen. He'd emailed Tyler a photograph of the obituary, and Tyler assured Mackinnon he would get DC Webb to look into it straight away. They needed to track down where it had been published and who paid for the obituary notice. If they found out who had paid for the notice, that could be the breakthrough they needed in identifying Beverley Madison's killer.

Tyler had told Mackinnon that the snake venom had been identified as being from a Russell's viper.

Mackinnon didn't know much about snakes. In fact, he'd always had a bit of a phobia of snakes. Reptiles in general really. But identifying the type of snake used to kill Beverley Madison was good progress. It meant they could track down whoever owned Russell's vipers in the UK, or whether it was possible to purchase the venom. Mackinnon wouldn't be surprised. It seemed like you could buy anything on the Internet these days.

Mackinnon flicked the indicator and changed lanes, anticipating the junction ahead.

He turned up the heating. It was a cold and wet December evening. Chloe would probably be getting home by now, and she was expecting Mackinnon to be there for dinner. He would have to ring her as soon as he got back to the station. There was no way he'd be able to get back to Oxford tonight. He would have to stay at Derek's. Unfortunately, it looked like he had a long night ahead of him.

CHAPTER FIFTEEN

I RUSHED HOME AFTER WORK, eager to have enough time to finalise my plans. I opened the gate in front of my semi-detached house and walked along the garden path. I glanced at the house next door and saw Gillian Rice peering at me from behind her net curtains.

Great. That was all I needed. I hurried along, hoping to get inside before she accosted me.

I put my key in the lock… so close.

"Yoo-hoo," a shrill voice said.

I turned to my left and saw Gillian Rice standing there, holding a transparent umbrella and leaning on the fence that separated our two properties.

"How are you, dear?" she asked. "I haven't seen your mother in a while?"

I let out a shaky breath. I was running on pure adrenaline. I didn't know whether it was nerves or excitement, but either way, I needed to get rid of Gillian Rice and get on with my plans.

I knew Gillian had heard the gossip. I'd seen her looking out of her bedroom window when the care home's van came to pick up my mother.

I could never forget Gillian's disapproving eyes fixed on me the night the ambulance had arrived. I shivered, remembering how I'd arrived home from work to find my mother cradling her scalded hands.

Gillian blamed me.

"She is still in hospital," I said, not wanting to get into the whys and wherefores with Gillian now.

"Oh dear," Gillian said. "How awful. She must have been far more seriously injured than I thought."

I hated Gillian Rice.

I was standing there, getting soaking wet. The rain was trickling down my neck. She stood there, nice and dry with her cheap transparent umbrella, trying to pry and find out what had happened to my mother.

Nosey cow!

I raised my hand again to turn the key, but my hands were shaking. I was so furious with her, but I couldn't afford to lose control tonight. I had too much work to do.

I forced myself to smile politely at Gillian.

"She's getting better," I said. "Hopefully, she'll be coming home soon."

Gillian nodded sagely. "I hope so. I was saying to Alfred only yesterday that we hadn't seen your mother in such a long time."

Her eyes flickered to the upstairs of my house as though

she thought I had my mother stashed up there. Perhaps she thought I had her locked in a bedroom.

Did she think I was some kind of monster?

Maybe I was.

"Good night, Gillian," I said firmly. I opened the front door, stepped inside and slammed it behind me.

I took a few seconds to try and calm down. People made mistakes when they were anxious, and I couldn't afford to make any mistakes, not yet.

Bloody Gillian. I could just picture her when this was all over, preening for the TV crews and telling them she'd always suspected I was evil.

I switched on the hallway light, shrugged off my coat and stepped inside the living room.

My hands were still shaking as I reached for the pack of matches on the mahogany cabinet, but somehow I managed to light one and hold it to the wick of the candle.

The candlelight flickered and illuminated the framed photographs I'd arranged carefully on the sideboard. I took a moment to look down at the photos and focus.

It didn't take long before a feeling of calm flooded through me. I felt strong again, the photos strengthening my resolve.

I took a quick glance at the clock on the mantelpiece. It had been given to my father at his retirement party. After forty years' service at the same company, he retired and all he got was that clock. Two weeks later, he was dead. They said it was a heart attack that was probably brought on by his high blood pressure, but I knew the truth.

It was the stress that had killed him.

* * *

Ninety minutes later, I had changed into black Lycra leggings and an oversized sweatshirt. I also wore my hooded coat and as I strode across the car park, I pulled the hood low over my face. It was still raining so the hood wouldn't raise anyone's suspicions.

It paid to do your homework. And I was good at it. Methodical and precise. I'd had this target in my sights for weeks, and I knew his routine like the back of my hand.

I pushed open the doors to the gym and strode by the reception desk confidently, as if I knew exactly where I was going.

I made as if I was going to enter the ladies changing rooms, but at the last minute, after a quick glance over my shoulder to make sure no one was looking, I turned right into the empty office area.

I glanced at the clock on the wall. I didn't have long. In a few minutes, he would be finishing the last fitness class of the evening. I made a grab for the car keys on the desk. Silly place to keep them, but it made my task easier.

I shoved them into the pocket of my coat. Keeping my hood pulled up, I stepped out into the corridor again and walked past a group of women enquiring about a new spinning class.

My heart was thudding in my chest, and I wanted to run. I forced myself to walk slowly. I didn't want to attract any unwanted attention.

Outside the gym, I walked across the car park, heading for a small silver Peugeot. I pressed the button on the key fob, and the car beeped and unlocked. I smiled, shoved the keys into my pocket again and headed back towards the gym.

There was a CCTV camera in the car park not far from the Peugeot. I wasn't sure if it worked or whether it was one of those dummy ones places like this used to give people a false sense of security and deter break-ins. Real or not, I didn't want to take any chances, and I kept my gaze focused on the floor and my hood pulled down low.

Getting the keys back to the office was almost as easy. The same group of women were still hovering by the reception desk, so I was easily able to slip my way past them unnoticed, but this time there were two men standing right beside the door to the office. They were identically dressed in very short blue shorts and white socks pulled halfway up their calves. I hesitated for a moment, hoping they would make their way either into the gym or into the changing rooms. But they didn't. They seemed quite content to stay exactly where they were for a chat.

I bit down so hard on the inside of my mouth that I tasted blood. This wasn't part of the plan. I didn't have time for this. I didn't want anyone to see me going in the office, but I had to take a chance. He would be back soon.

Deciding it was my only option, I kept my head down as I stepped past the two idiots. I slipped inside the office, dropped the keys back on the desk. Then I spun around and walked back past the reception as fast as my legs could carry me.

I turned back just as I got outside, but none of them were watching me. I stared at them through the huge rain-splattered glass panes. They really had no idea.

I tried to slow my breathing. It was fine, I reassured

myself. Everything was going to plan. It was time to move on to stage two.

I went back to the Peugeot and opened the back door. I slipped into the rear passenger seat and closed the door behind me. Out of my pocket, I pulled a small plastic container, which contained my syringe.

It wouldn't be long now.

I hunkered down behind the driver's seat. It wasn't easy. He was a tall man, and he had pushed his chair right back, but I had to put up with it.

It wouldn't be for long. He would notice if I moved the position of his seat and that wouldn't do at all. He wouldn't be quite as easy as Beverley Madison. I needed the element of surprise to make this work.

CHAPTER SIXTEEN

JOE GRIFFIN FORCED A SMILE when he saw Angela lurking beside the changing rooms after the class. He'd just taken an hour of circuits, and he was tired. All he wanted to do was get home, have a glass of wine and relax with his wife in front of the TV.

He walked briskly towards Angela, hoping to pass her and get out of there before she could strike up a conversation.

"That was a great class, Joe," she said, twirling a lock of her hair around her index finger.

"Thanks. Glad you enjoyed it," Joe said.

"I always love your classes," Angela said, sidling up to him. "And this class is so good for me. Here, feel this…" She held out her arm and braced it, grabbed Joe's hand and placed it on her bicep. "See what you've done to my body."

Joe pulled his hand away. "Fantastic result," he said.

"And just think, all that muscle will be burning more calories."

"Speaking of calories," Angela said, "do you fancy going for a drink or maybe getting some dinner tonight?"

Joe shook his head. "No can do, I'm afraid. Carla is waiting for me at home," he said, but mentioning his wife didn't seem to have any effect on Angela.

"Maybe some other time," she said moving even closer to him.

"Maybe," he said, extracting himself from Angela's grip and opening the door to the men's changing rooms. At least she couldn't follow him in there.

After a quick shower and change of clothes, Joe cautiously left the men's changing rooms. When Alison, the girl at reception, saw him scanning the corridor, she laughed. "It's all right. You're safe. She has gone home."

Joe sighed in relief. "Thank God," he said.

Joe lifted his gym kit onto his shoulder and said goodbye to Alison. He needed to be back in the gym tomorrow. Another seven am start. That was the problem with his type of job. As a personal trainer and fitness instructor, it meant he had to be available when clients wanted him. The highest demand was usually early morning or late evening. Before work and after work. Still, it was a satisfying job. He enjoyed helping people achieve their fitness goals — even if he did have to deal with annoying, touchy-feely women like Angela.

Joe headed towards his silver Peugeot. He opened the boot and threw his gym kit inside.

He slammed the door and walked around to the driver's side of the car, yawning. It had been a hell of a long day.

Joe slid into the driving seat. As soon as he shut the door, he felt a sharp sting on his neck. He jerked forward and turned around, clutching his neck.

Damn, that hurt.

He examined the headrest expecting to see an insect, but there was nothing there. He rubbed his neck with one hand as he reached up with the other to switch the interior light on.

He saw something on the floor. At first glance, he thought it was a pile of old clothes, but then he saw a pair of eyes gleaming at him.

Joe gave a strangled yelp and reached for the door handle.

Someone was in his car! What the hell?

"Get out of my car," Joe ordered, staggering out of the driver's seat and flinging the back passenger door open. "What did you just do? You scratched my neck."

There was no movement from the back seat.

"I'm warning you. Get out now, or I'll drag you out."

A figure emerged, bundled up in a winter coat.

Joe didn't notice the figure's face, and even if he'd lived long enough, he wouldn't have been able to give a description to the police. His eyes were fixed on the syringe, which shone in the gleam of the streetlight. Joe felt an unpleasant stinging pain in his neck and moaned in terror.

"What is that?" he pleaded. "What did you inject me with?"

A million thoughts flashed through his mind. Was this some weirdo with an infected needle...HIV or hepatitis?

A searing pain stabbed behind his eyes. Joe stepped

forward, making a grab for his tormentor, but the dark figure stepped out of his reach easily.

Joe stumbled and realised he needed to get help and fast. He patted down his pockets, looking for his mobile phone, but belatedly he realised it was in his gym bag in the boot of the car.

His best chance of getting help was heading back to the gym.

Still clutching his neck, Joe staggered back towards the lights of the gym, leaning on cars as he went. The figure made no attempt to stop him.

"I'm going to call the police, you crazy bastard," Joe shouted.

He was too far away to be sure, but Joe thought he heard the figure say, "No you won't, Joe. You'll never make it inside."

CHAPTER SEVENTEEN

AFTER MACKINNON GOT BACK TO Wood Street station, he filled Tyler in on the developments with Jacob Jansen. Tyler told him Hassan was exhibits officer on the case, so he left the obituary in DC Hassan's capable hands.

When he'd finished debriefing Tyler, Mackinnon headed outside to give Chloe a call. He had to tell her he wouldn't be home tonight. He was pretty sure Chloe wouldn't be pleased, and Mackinnon didn't want everyone else in the briefing room to overhear the conversation.

As he stepped outside, the wet chill of the December evening hit him, and he buttoned up his coat and turned his collar up. Hunching up his shoulders, he called the home phone.

Katy answered.

"Hi, sweetheart. Did you have a good day?"

Katy answered with a sigh, "Not really."

"What happened?"

Another sigh. "Just the usual," she said, her voice monotone and very unlike her normal cheerful self.

Mackinnon felt sorry for the kid. She'd been having trouble at school. A group of girls seemed to delight in teasing Katy, excluding her and generally making her feel awful.

"Have those girls been giving you trouble again? Your mum said if you give her their names, she'll speak to your headmistress."

Katy was silent. They'd had this conversation last week. She didn't want to tell Chloe the names of the girls who had been targeting her. Katy insisted it would only make matters worse, and to be honest, Mackinnon tended to agree with her.

"I suppose you're ringing to say you're going to be late," Katy said, in an almost perfect imitation of Chloe.

Mackinnon almost laughed.

"Worse than that, kiddo. This case I'm working on means that I won't be home tonight. I'm going to stay at Derek's. Is your mum around?"

"I'll get her."

Mackinnon looked up at the night sky. The misty rain fell softly on his face. He stepped closer to the building so he was under cover.

"Jack? Katy just told me you're not coming back tonight."

"I'm sorry. I'm going to stay at Derek's. It's this case. It's going to be a late one."

"Well, that's a shame," Chloe said. "I've got a bottle of your favourite red wine."

Mackinnon grinned. "Save it for me. I'll be back tomorrow."

"You sure?"

"Pretty sure," Mackinnon said, not wanting to give any promises he couldn't keep.

"All right, fair enough," Chloe said. "It'll keep. But do try and get home tomorrow, Jack. I could really do with a chat."

"What about?"

"Have you got time to talk now?"

"I've got a few minutes before the next briefing," Mackinnon said. "What's wrong?"

"Nothing new," Chloe said. "It's Katy. I'm getting really worried about her. She won't tell me exactly what's wrong, but she keeps saying that she wants to leave her school and go to another one."

"Perhaps that's not a bad idea," Mackinnon said

"It's an excellent school, Jack. And she's going to be doing her GCSEs next year. I just don't want her to screw up her future because she's fallen out with a couple of girls in her year."

"Katy doesn't really seem the type to over dramatise things." Mackinnon thought that if it had been Sarah they were discussing, he might have agreed with Chloe.

But Katy usually got on with things, and he didn't think she would be kicking up such a fuss if she wasn't really unhappy.

But Chloe knew Katy better than he did. "Why don't we try and speak to her again tomorrow night when I come home? We can all have dinner together. If she can explain exactly why she wants to leave…" Mackinnon heard the sound of liquid glugging into a glass. "I hope that's not my wine you're drinking," Mackinnon teased.

"Might be," Chloe said, and he could tell from her voice she was smiling. "I'll get you another one."

"I'd better get back upstairs. The briefing starts soon, and Tyler will be looking for me."

"Okay, speak to you later."

"Jack?" Chloe said just as he was about to hang up.

"Yes?"

"Be careful, won't you?"

After Mackinnon hung up, he sent a text to Derek to ask if he could crash at his place that night. Mackinnon had his own set of keys, and Derek had told him he could come and go as he pleased, but Mackinnon still liked to give him fair warning.

Mackinnon had just pressed the send button when Collins walked outside. "Charlotte said you came out here," Collins said. He was only in his suit jacket. He crossed his arms over his chest and shivered. "It's bloody freezing out here. What are you doing?"

"I just needed some fresh air," Mackinnon said, checking his watch. "I'm not late, am I? We still have five minutes before the briefing starts."

He started to walk back towards the station entrance.

"The briefing has been delayed," Collins said. "But we'd better get back inside."

Mackinnon frowned. Collins' face looked tense. "What's happened?"

"We've got another one," Collins said.

Mackinnon followed Collins upstairs as he took the stairs two at a time. The incident room was a hub of activity when they reached it, phones ringing, people calling to each other over the desks.

DI Tyler strode across the room and met Mackinnon's gaze.

"We've got another victim," he said. "This time they've been sloppy. They left the syringe at the scene. They are going to regret that mistake."

"Where?" Mackinnon asked.

"Fast Fitness. A gym on Hale Street, round the back of London Bridge station. He was found in the car park."

"It's a male victim this time?" Mackinnon frowned. Different location and completely different type of victim. Unpredictable. That wasn't good.

"Another body in less than twenty four hours," Collins said. "Christ."

Tyler nodded. "My sentiments exactly. You and Mackinnon get yourselves over to the scene. I'll follow you over there after I've briefed DCI Brookbank."

CHAPTER EIGHTEEN

BY THE TIME MACKINNON AND Collins got to the scene, it was already a hub of activity. A dark corner of the car park at the front of the Fast Fitness gym was illuminated with lights. A section of the car park had been sealed off, and there was a group of gym members who were arguing furiously with a uniformed officer standing by the tape. They wanted their cars back, but they wouldn't get them until they had been interviewed.

Mackinnon took a moment to help the harassed uniformed officer by explaining to the crowd that they would not be able to access their cars and should wait inside the gym for questioning. There were a few stragglers, but most did as he asked and returned to the gym.

Sheets of tarpaulin blocked the view of the body from members of the public who were hanging around by the tape.

DI Tyler arrived just minutes after Collins and Mackinnon. He was talking to the crime scene manager when Mackinnon wandered over. He nodded, and as Tyler continued his conversation with the crime scene manager, Mackinnon suited up, slipping on pale blue covers over his own shoes, so he didn't contaminate the crime scene.

It was bitingly cold, but at least the rain had stopped.

Tyler looked up as Mackinnon approached. "We've got some differences this time," he said.

"Are we sure it's the same killer?" Mackinnon asked. From where he stood, he could see the victim was a well-built man, and there was no sign of bloating as there had been on Beverley Madison's body.

"They left the syringe this time," Tyler said. "It's got to be the same one."

"He was a big bloke," Mackinnon said. "Can't have been easy to overpower him."

"There's no sign of a struggle at all, is there?"

Mackinnon looked at the crime scene manager, who shook his head.

Tyler sighed and rubbed his temples with his fingertips. "I'm thinking perhaps he was taken by surprise. I don't know how quickly this venom works. From what DC Brown learned talking to a specialist at the London School of Hygiene and Tropical Medicine, if it was a normal bite from a snake it could kill in a matter of minutes. But injecting the venom by syringe means much more venom can be delivered, more than a typical snakebite. So death probably comes very quickly."

Mackinnon edged closer for another look at the victim. He guessed the man was about his own age. He was tall, over six-foot and well-built.

DI Tyler finished his conversation with the crime scene manager and joined Mackinnon by the body.

"What have we got on him so far?" Mackinnon asked.

Tyler puffed out a breath. "Collins has gone to talk to the caretaker. He's the one who called it in. Poor bloke. He's a bit shaken up. A woman called Leslie Green found the body an hour ago, and her screams alerted the caretaker who patrols the grounds every hour or so. They've had problems with thieves breaking into cars, so they put up some more of these lights recently," Tyler gestured with a nod to a yellow-tinted lamp a couple of metres away. "There is also working CCTV." He pointed to the camera in the corner of the car park. "We're getting a copy of the footage now, but from what we've seen so far we've got a hooded figure running away. It's not going to help us much. Collins is trying to talk with Leslie Green, but I'm not sure how much we can get out of her. She didn't see the killer. She only found the body lying on the floor."

"What's his name?" Mackinnon said, staring down at the dead man.

"Joe Griffin. A local boy. Works as a personal trainer, and he has worked here for about five years, according to the woman on the reception desk. According to colleagues we've spoken to, he was a friendly chap, not the type to have enemies."

Tyler waved over one of the uniformed officers. "PC Green," he said. "How many members of staff have you managed to speak to so far?"

PC Green looked nervous. He cleared his throat. "Erm, let me see…I've managed to talk to the lady on reception, as well as a woman who took the evening step class and to one of the cleaners. They're on a skeleton staff tonight. They were meant to have five staff on rota, but one called in sick. Some sort of bug going around apparently."

"What did they tell you about the victim?"

"They all seem in agreement, saying that he was a pleasant man, easy to get along with. Although, he had a bit of a flirtation thing going on with a couple of the female clients."

Tyler looked at Mackinnon and raised an eyebrow. "Maybe he was playing around?"

"You think an angry husband did this?" Mackinnon shook his head. "What on earth links him with Beverley Madison?"

PC Green perked up, and his eyes widened. "Do you think it had something to do with the Charmer then, sir?"

Tyler pulled a face and looked at PC Green. "The Charmer? Where on earth do you get these things?"

PC Green flushed. "It's what everyone is calling him. You know…like a snake charmer."

Tyler glared at him. "I'll speak to you later." Tyler dismissed him by turning his back.

"Have you ever heard anything so ridiculous?" Tyler said to Mackinnon.

"I think we've got Jacob Jansen to thank for that. He mentioned it to the press when I was there."

"Bloody idiot," Tyler muttered.

"So where do we go from here? It's going to be a while before the crime scene unit have finished."

"I'm going to stick around," Tyler said. "I've got Collins talking to Lesley Green and the caretaker, trying to find out if either of them saw anything relevant."

Tyler hesitated and looked up at Mackinnon, then said, "I'd like you to go and talk to Joe Griffin's wife, Jack."

Mackinnon felt the beginnings of indigestion start to burn in his chest. He hated giving death messages. But it was a necessary evil. He nodded.

"Her name is Carla Griffin." Tyler gave Mackinnon the address.

Mackinnon headed off, ducking beneath the tape and making his way towards his own car. Collins would have to get a lift back with Tyler.

As soon as Mackinnon slipped into the driver's seat, he felt in his coat pocket for an indigestion tablet. He slipped it in his mouth and leaned back for a second with his eyes closed.

After taking a deep breath, he leaned forward and started the car.

He was about to ruin Carla Griffin's life.

CHAPTER NINETEEN

MACKINNON SAT IN THE SMALL front room in the terraced house that had belonged to Joe Griffin. Opposite him, Carla Griffin sat pale and horrified on the sofa, surrounded by bright pink cushions.

This was the worst bit. After delivering the devastating news, Mackinnon then had to stay and ask prying questions about Joe Griffin's life. He had to grill her about the state of their marriage and ask whether she thought anyone had wished her husband harm.

He'd met up with the family liaison officer, Kristin Murphy, on the street outside the small terraced house.

Carla Griffin had opened the door with a smile. She was in the middle of a sentence, laughing as she assumed it was Joe and asking him if he had forgotten his key.

The smile had slid from her face when she saw Mackinnon and Kristin standing there.

She had been silent at first, and then after she had processed the initial bombshell, she'd cried. But she hadn't gotten angry yet. That stage of grief was still to come. Right now, she was still too shocked to feel much of anything.

Kristin entered the small living room, holding mugs of tea. Mackinnon took his with a murmur of thanks. Kristin had to hold the mug up to Carla for a few seconds before Carla even realised she was there.

Eventually, Carla blinked up at her and grasped the handle.

"Are you sure it's Joe," she said. "It might not be him. He works late sometimes." She looked up at Mackinnon with a painful half smile, but the hope didn't quite reach her eyes.

"We believe it is Joe," Mackinnon said carefully. "A number of his colleagues saw him, and they identified him."

"I don't understand," she said, shaking her head. "How did it happen? Was he mugged?"

"We are investigating your husband's death, Mrs. Griffin," Mackinnon said. "But we don't believe it was a mugging. We think it's possible your husband may have been deliberately targeted by someone. Is there anyone you can think of who might have wanted to harm Joe?"

Carla's eyes filled with tears. "No, not Joe. Everyone loves Joe."

Carla started to shiver and Kristin perched on the sofa beside her and leaned forward to pat her hand. "Can I get you a cardi? Something to keep you warm. You've had a terrible shock."

Carla stared straight ahead. "No. I'm not cold." She

didn't stop shivering.

Mackinnon glanced around the room, taking in the framed photographs on the mantelpiece. In pride of place at the centre was a large photograph of Joe and Carla on their wedding day, looking happy and hopeful for the future.

Sometimes life could be so unfair.

"Is there someone who could come and stay with you?" Kristin asked. "Your mum or another family member perhaps?"

Carla turned to face Kristin. "Yes, my mum."

"Okay, good."

Carla's fingers interlaced around the mug of tea she held on her lap. She was shaking so badly that some of the tea spilled. She didn't even flinch when Kristin artfully removed the mug and laid it down on the coffee table.

Suddenly Carla's eyes filled with fresh tears. "I'm going to have to tell Joe's mum and dad, aren't I? Oh God, I can't do that."

Kristin put a comforting hand on Carla's shoulder. "Don't worry about that," she said. "If it helps, I can do it for you."

Carla nodded but then she took a shaky breath and said, "No, I've got to do it. I don't want a stranger telling them about Joe."

Mackinnon decided to ask a couple more questions then finish up. He had asked Carla all the questions he could think of, and she was too shocked at this stage to answer in detail. They would have to try again tomorrow.

"How had Joe been acting recently? Had he been stressed or worried about anything?"

Carla shook her head. "No, nothing. We were happy. We

were planning a holiday in Barbados in February. I suppose I'll have to cancel it now."

"This is a sensitive question, Mrs. Griffin," Mackinnon said, thinking about the obituary that Beverley Madison had received before her death. "Had your husband received anything, any notes or any threats recently?"

Mackinnon was expecting Carla to repeat her statement that everyone loved Joe, but she didn't.

She bit her lip and then folded her arms. "There weren't any threats as such, but there was something."

She looked up and frowned as if she was trying hard to remember something. She got to her feet and walked across to a pine cabinet, pulling open one drawer after another until she found what she was looking for. Finally after rummaging around, she pulled out a small square of paper.

Mackinnon held his breath.

He knew what it was even before Carla had showed it to him.

"It was horrible. Joe got it in the post last week. I thought we should tell the police, but he said it was just some idiot playing a practical joke."

Kristin stared wide-eyed at Mackinnon as they waited for Carla to continue.

"I didn't think it was funny at all. But Joe said I was overreacting." She handed the small piece of paper to Mackinnon. It was an obituary notice, torn from a newspaper, just like the one sent to Beverley Madison.

Carla wrapped her arms around her chest and hugged herself tightly. She bit down on her lip, then said, "Do you think it was a warning?" Her voice cracked. "What does it mean?"

"I'm not sure yet," Mackinnon said. "But we are going to do everything we can to find out who killed your husband. I promise."

CHAPTER TWENTY

WHEN MACKINNON FINALLY GOT HOME, it was almost two in the morning. He wasn't expecting Derek to be up. As he let himself in with his key, Molly, Derek's Border Collie gave a warning bark.

"Hey, sweetheart, keep quiet. It's only me," Mackinnon said in a whisper.

He headed straight for the kitchen and poured himself a glass of water. As he drained the glass, he spotted a note from Derek on the kitchen counter.

Curry in fridge. You're welcome.

Mackinnon grinned. Good old Derek. Mackinnon felt his stomach rumble. He hadn't eaten since the bacon sandwich he'd had for breakfast.

He opened the refrigerator and pulled out two foil trays, one containing pilau rice, the other containing Mackinnon's favourite: lamb rogan josh.

Mackinnon had just started to pile the curry on a plate when he heard a movement behind him.

He turned to see Derek scratching his head, his eyes bleary from sleep.

"Sorry," Mackinnon said. "I didn't mean to wake you. Thanks for this." He pointed at the curry.

Derek yawned. "You are all right. It was Molly who woke me up," he said, leaning forward to scratch the dog behind her ears.

"Bad night?" Derek asked.

Mackinnon put the plate into the microwave and turned it on. He leaned back against the kitchen counter and nodded. "Pretty bad. There was no way I could have gone back to Oxford tonight and then been back in London for an early start in the morning. Thanks for letting me crash here."

"No problem," Derek said.

"I thought you might be staying at Julia's tonight."

Derek shrugged. "Yeah. That's over."

Mackinnon raised an eyebrow. "I thought things were going well."

"So did I. I guess I was wrong."

Mackinnon wasn't terribly surprised. Derek's girlfriends never stuck around for long, although it tended to be Derek who grew tired of being in a relationship and shrank away from commitment.

"She dumped you then?" Mackinnon asked.

Derek scowled. "Don't spare my feelings, will you?" He sighed. "It was just all this talk of Christmas. She wanted me to spend it with her parents and kept dropping hints about a certain item of jewellery for Christmas."

Derek shuddered. "She was moving too fast."

Mackinnon took his plate out of the microwave and stirred the lamb curry before shoving it back in and putting it on for another minute.

"Maybe you could have told her that you thought things were moving too fast. She might have been happy to slow things down."

Derek shook his head and looked at Mackinnon as if he was crazy. "That wouldn't have worked. Once she got that idea in her head, there was no slowing things down. A clean break is best for everyone."

Mackinnon shrugged. "You okay, though?"

Derek nodded. "I'm fine."

Derek didn't normally waste any energy on regretting past relationships, but this one seemed a little different. He'd been with Julia for a while now. Mackinnon had started to think she might have been the one.

As the microwave pinged, Derek yawned again. "Right. I'm going back to bed. Enjoy the curry."

"I will," Mackinnon said. "Thanks again."

He put his plate on a tray and carried it over to the sofa. He switched on the TV to watch the news. Molly curled up by his feet.

Mackinnon had just taken his first bite of lamb, which was fantastic as always, when the story on Sky news changed.

The Charmer was flashed across the screen in huge letters, and recorded images of the crime scene in the car park outside Fast Fitness played behind the newsreader.

Mackinnon groaned. Great. DI Tyler would be in a foul mood tomorrow.

CHAPTER TWENTY-ONE

CHARLOTTE RUBBED HER EYES AND then leaned back in the chair, staring up at the bright fluorescent lights overhead. She was going to have to call it a day soon. She'd been trawling through the dangerous wild animal licences from the local councils. She needed to discover if anyone had a licence for a Russell's viper. Of course it was a long shot. The killer could be someone who owned a snake illegally, or perhaps they just bought the venom from someone else. Maybe it was naive to hope that the killer had done things legally.

She took a sip of her coffee, which had grown cold ages ago, and then stared at her computer screen. It was making her eyes sting. She'd been looking at the damn thing for so long.

As she made a note of one of the names, a thought that had been running around her head all day struck her again.

There were so many easier ways to kill people. This had to be some kind of statement.

Why were they using snakes, and why a Russell's viper in particular? She'd been instructed to approach the process logically by looking through the licences, but there was another way to come at this problem. A way that Charlotte thought would give them a better chance of success.

Handling snakes like this was a risky business. They might be after a deranged killer, but even deranged killers had self-preservation tendencies which meant surely they would want a supply of antivenom to hand.

If they were handling such a venomous snake, they would definitely want a supply handy. Charlotte made a note to look at suppliers of antivenom. If she could get a list of suppliers, and then see who they had sent antivenom to recently, she might get lucky.

Charlotte smiled. That made sense. Even if the killer wasn't holding the snakes legally and didn't have the Dangerous Wild Animals Licence, she still had a chance of tracking them through the antivenom.

Charlotte threw down her pen and grinned, pleased with her idea.

She searched the Internet, looking through suppliers of antivenom that shipped to the UK, and started to make a list. But twenty minutes later, she felt her eyelids drooping, and she knew she had to finish up for the night. She would get back to it first thing tomorrow morning.

She called a cab, and five minutes later, grabbed her coat and bag and switched off the lights as she left. As soon as she stepped outside Wood Street station, bundled up in her winter coat, she saw her cab pull up. She used a firm local to her, which was based in the East End.

She recognised the driver, Johnny, and smiled.

As she walked towards the taxi, she had the uncanny feeling that she was being watched. She turned and scanned the dark shadows. The skin prickled on the back of her neck, but she couldn't see anyone.

She slipped into the back of the cab and said hello to Johnny. She looked over her shoulder, out of the back window. She'd been sure that someone had been watching her.

But when Johnny pulled the taxi away from the curb and headed towards the East End, Charlotte forced herself to relax.

CHAPTER TWENTY-TWO

WHEN MACKINNON WOKE THE NEXT morning to the beeping of the alarm on his mobile phone, he groaned. It was five thirty in the morning, and he really didn't want to get up. He was cocooned in the warm duvet. The bedroom was freezing. Derek's central heating didn't come on for another hour.

He forced himself to get out of bed, shivering, and when he made his way into the equally cold bathroom and glanced in the mirror, he winced. His face showed every hour of sleep he hadn't had last night.

He stepped into the shower, and the hot water slowly made him feel more human. He headed straight out as soon as he'd dressed, not bothering to eat breakfast or even get a coffee. He could do that at the station.

He took the underground to work, travelling on one of the first trains. The underground was quiet at this time of the morning, and it was nice to get on a train and not feel like he was in a sardine can.

As soon as he came above ground and swiped his Oyster card at the barrier, he felt his phone buzzing in his pocket. He reached for it and saw Chloe's name flashing on the screen.

"Morning, sweetheart. You're up early."

"Jack," she said, and he could tell by that single word that she was tense. "Katy is refusing to go to school. She won't get out of bed, and she is supposed to be in early today for rehearsals."

"I know how she feels," Mackinnon said. "I didn't want to get up either. It's cold this morning."

"It's not that. It's this whole bullying problem. She's refusing to go to school. She's said she is never going back there. Nothing I say is getting through to her. Can you have a word?"

"I can try, but I'm not sure what good it will do. Why would she listen to me if she doesn't listen to you?"

"It's worth a try. I'm at my wits' end," Chloe said, and Mackinnon heard her steps on the stairs.

She said, "Here, you can talk to Jack and explain why you're not going to school today."

"I'm not going and you can't make me!" Katy's voice came through the phone loud and clear.

Mackinnon moved the phone a centimetre or so away from his ear. "Look," he said. "I know you're trying to convince your mum that you need to go to another school. But you've got to act like an adult about it, otherwise you won't get anywhere. I'll tell you what, I'll come home tonight and we will all have dinner together and talk it over properly."

Katy was silent on the other end of the phone.

"Come on. One more day, and we'll have a proper conversation about it tonight. I promise you we will listen to your point of view. Your mum isn't trying to do this to hurt you, Katy. She just wants what's best for you."

"This school isn't best for me," Katy snapped.

"Okay, so we'll talk about that tonight, and you can explain why it isn't the best choice for you, and why it's a good idea for you to go to another school."

"Will you be on my side?" Katy asked.

"I'm not going to be on anybody's side," Mackinnon said. "But I promise that your mum and I will both listen tonight. What do you say? One more day at school and then we can talk about it tonight?"

Katy sighed. "Okay, then. But only one more day."

When Katy hung up, Mackinnon was nearly at work, so rather than call Chloe back, he sent her a quick text message, telling her he'd be home that night for a family dinner and they could talk to Katy about the problem with the school.

As he walked past a newsstand, he caught a glimpse of the *Daily Record*. The front page was covered with the story of The Charmer. Mackinnon grabbed a copy.

He turned into Love Lane and saw Wood Street station ahead of him with its traditional police lamps outside.

It was still dark and it would be for another couple of hours yet. Mackinnon hated winter. He couldn't wait until the days got longer again. Maybe after Christmas he might book a holiday somewhere warm. Right now, he'd settle for anywhere that didn't cause his teeth to chatter from the cold.

* * *

DI Tyler had called an early morning briefing, and as he looked around the major incident room, Mackinnon thought most of the team looked as tired as he felt. Tyler sat at the head of the large table, and the rest of the major incident team took their seats around the table. Some of the civilian support staff and indexers who had come in early this morning were also in the room. A few had pulled in chairs from the room next door, and a couple of them leaned back against the wall as there wasn't space for everyone to sit down around the table.

DI Tyler looked shattered, Mackinnon thought. The strands of his grey hair were wet as though he had just splashed water on his face to try and wake up.

"Obituaries," Tyler said, jabbing his finger at the scanned image in front of him.

DC Webb was handing around files to everyone. The files contained images and detailed the developments in the case.

"So far the only link we have between the victims is the fact that they both had obituaries sent to them before they died. Someone is playing with them, tipping them off. Apparently, Joe Griffin didn't think it was worth worrying about, according to his wife Carla, and we know that Beverley Madison had assumed that Jacob Jansen sent her the obituary." Tyler leaned back in his chair and sighed.

"We can't find any link between Jacob Jansen and Joe Griffin," DC Collins said.

"I can't emphasise enough how important it is to find a link between our victims, Beverley Madison and Joe Griffin. Without it, we are really going to struggle with this investigation. DC Webb have you got anything to report back?"

DC Webb straightened in his chair and tapped his hand against his notepad. He had been assigned the task of tracking down the source of the obituaries.

"I haven't found out where they were printed yet. I'm working on the assumption that it was a local paper, and I have a list that I'm working my way through. Some of them are online, which should make matters easier, but there are a surprising number of local papers out there."

"Well, keep at it," Tyler said. "Once we know which newspaper published these obituaries, we can find out who paid for them and that should lead us to our culprit."

"Collins?" Tyler prompted.

DC Collins smothered a yawn and put down his cup of coffee, focusing his attention on his notes. "I've been going through the statements. We still have some gaps in Joe Griffin's timeline. I need to speak to a couple of other people who attended Joe Griffin's classes at the gym."

Tyler nodded and turned his attention to Charlotte who smiled confidently.

"I've been going through the lists we received regarding the dangerous wild animals act and making a shortlist of those people who had been granted licences in this area."

"Waste of time," DC Webb muttered.

DI Tyler looked up sharply. "We can't dismiss anything. We have to be thorough."

"Well, it's hardly likely if he was planning to use the venom to kill someone that he would have registered a poisonous snake in his name."

Evie Charlesworth, who was standing at the back of the room holding a pen and notebook, said, "Actually snakes aren't poisonous. They're venomous."

DC Webb screwed up his face. "What?"

"There's a difference," Evie insisted. "They are not poisonous."

"All right," DC Webb said irritably. "So they are venomous. That doesn't change the fact we are unlikely to be dealing with someone stupid enough to register the fact they've got a snake."

"You might be right," Charlotte said. "I was thinking about this last night, even if they didn't want to register the fact they had a dangerous snake, they would need one thing."

Tyler looked up from his notes. "And what is that?"

"Antivenom," Charlotte said. "Whoever our killer is we know that they are dealing with a highly dangerous toxin. If it was me, handling something like that, I'd like to have a safety net. I'd want to have antivenom on hand just in case."

"That makes sense." Tyler nodded. "So we need to look into suppliers of antivenom over the last six months."

Charlotte nodded. "I've started to compile a list of suppliers. We might need a warrant to get the information that we need from them."

Tyler nodded. "Won't be a problem. Good work."

After assigning a few more actions to the team and

making sure that everybody knew their role in the investigation, Tyler set down the file on the desk in front of him.

"I can't emphasise this enough. We need to find a connection between our victims." Tyler looked steadily at each individual sitting around the table. "There's no way this is random," he said. "It can't be."

CHAPTER TWENTY-THREE

AFTER THE BRIEFING, MACKINNON GRABBED a cup of coffee and ordered a bacon roll to go from the canteen. He ate his breakfast as he walked in the direction of Moorgate station. He had an appointment with the reptile expert at London zoo. There was no point driving. He knew it would be far quicker to get there using public transport.

He left the underground at Camden Town and walked along Camden High Street towards Regent's Park and the London zoo.

Mackinnon arrived at the zoo just after it opened at ten am. The cold, miserable December day meant there were fewer tourists than usual gathered around the entrance. Mackinnon was able to gain access quickly by showing his warrant card at one of the turnstiles.

He was escorted by one of the zoo's employees, a young man dressed all in khaki, to the reptile house. He'd expected to go into the viewing area, but instead, the young man led Mackinnon around the back of the building to the research centre.

The outside of the building was covered in wood, a decorative effect for the tourists' benefit. The building was actually modern and made of brick. Mackinnon was glad of that. He didn't like the idea of anything in there escaping.

He'd been reluctant when Tyler first asked him to go and speak to the snake expert. Mackinnon wasn't exactly enamoured with snakes. He didn't hate them, but that didn't mean he wanted to get any closer than he had to.

He was greeted by Claude Peterson, an enthusiastic South African, who was the head of the reptile centre. Claude was only slightly shorter than Mackinnon. He had long hair that reached his shoulders but was thinning on top. His face was lined in a way that made it obvious he was someone who spent a great deal of time in the sun.

Claude pushed up his sleeves and held out a hand to shake Mackinnon's.

Mackinnon noticed the snake tattoo on Claude's right forearm.

"I got it when I was drunk," Claude said with a laugh. "Now, how can I help you? We don't often have detectives paying visits to our reptile centre."

"I have a few questions I hope you can answer," Mackinnon said. "About a snake known as the Russell's viper."

"Not a snake to be messed with," Claude said. "But one to be admired. Here, come inside. I'll show you our research lab."

He opened the internal door and led Mackinnon into a

large open-plan area. It was kitted out like a laboratory, but on every wall, there were huge, glass tanks, containing heating lamps and various types of foliage and rocks.

Mackinnon looked at the one closest to him. At first he thought it was empty, until he saw a slight movement out of the corner of his eye. He flinched.

Claude laughed. "I see you're not too keen on snakes, eh?"

"I can't say they're my favourite animals," Mackinnon said. "I'm more of a dog man."

Claude laughed again. "I hear that a lot, but the snakes aren't really so bad. They're quite a marvel of nature.

"We have actually helped many people overcome their phobias. I could get you to hold one if you like? Maybe a harmless corn snake. Just a small one."

Mackinnon shook his head. "No, thanks. I prefer to see them in their cases like this."

"Fair enough," Claude said. "There is something sensible and healthy about having a fear of snakes. In most people, it's an inbuilt fear."

Mackinnon nodded. He could relate to that.

"It is scientifically based," Claude said. "If you think about it, in order to survive out in the wild, it makes sense to be afraid and try to avoid snakes."

Mackinnon nodded again. It certainly made sense to him.

"This particular little beauty," Claude said, leaning down and gazing at the dark snake with the bright green pattern. "She is a spitting snake. Fairly dangerous as she actually spits the venom into your eyes."

Mackinnon was very glad the Perspex was separating him from the snake.

"They don't want to hurt us," Claude said. "For them, it is just a matter of survival."

He took a step forward and then pointed to another of the cases.

"This one is my favourite," he said to Mackinnon. "This one is a King Cobra."

The snake he was looking at didn't have the same spectacular markings of the spitting snake, but its sheer size was impressive.

"Isn't she a beauty?" Claude asked.

The snake remained motionless, its cold eyes fixed on Mackinnon.

"She is quite a large snake," Mackinnon said. He didn't agree with Claude Peterson's assessment, but he didn't want to offend him.

Claude smirked. "It was the Russell's viper you asked me about." He perched on a stool and gestured to the one next to him for Mackinnon to do the same. "I have some pictures for you. We don't have one here right now. They are very... Look!" Claude said, looking over Mackinnon's shoulder and pointing to the case behind him. "She is moving."

Mackinnon tensed and turned to see the King Cobra slowly shift its position and uncoil its massive body.

Claude laughed at Mackinnon's response. "I suppose now is not a good time to tell you that we had one escape from its enclosure?"

"Recently?" Mackinnon asked.

"No," Claude shook his head. "It was a pit viper making a bid for freedom. Somehow it managed to escape. We got into some trouble over that and had to fill out a hell of a lot of paperwork. We still don't know how she managed it."

Claude grinned and stood up. "Here, let me show you something I have set up." Claude walked across to a lab bench at the far side of the room, and Mackinnon followed.

Claude slipped on a pair of latex gloves and then he picked up a pipette. He drew up a small amount of straw coloured liquid from a vial and then reached across to pick up a small container of red liquid.

Claude turned to smile at Mackinnon and held up the container. "This is blood. It's not human, it would have the same effect if it was, though. Now, watch this…"

He angled the pipette and squirted a tiny drop of the liquid into the blood. Almost instantaneously, the mixture changed. Claude put down his pipette and held up the container of blood.

He shook it from side to side. The blood had turned into a gelatinous mess.

"You see," Claude said. "The blood cells have clumped together forming this jellylike substance. The venom promotes coagulation — clotting."

Claude showed Mackinnon photographs of the Russell's viper, spreading them out on the lab bench.

"We know that the victims are not being bitten by snakes," Mackinnon said. "Somehow the venom is being extracted and then injected into the victims."

Claude nodded. "That's even more dangerous. Some snakes are known to give a dry bite. That's when the snake will bite, but doesn't inject venom. And some snakes have highly potent venom but they only inject a very small amount at a time. By injecting an entire syringe full of venom..." Claude gave a low whistle and shrugged. "Do you know the exact volume used?"

Mackinnon shook his head and Claude nodded. "I would guess it would be more than you would get from a normal snakebite, and so it would work faster and be more likely to be fatal."

"We are looking into how someone might be able to get hold of this venom. Would they need to have a snake? Or would they be able to buy it from somewhere?"

Claude frowned. "There's a process known as milking," he said. "That is where you milk a snake of its venom and retain it in a suitable container."

Claude must've noticed the discomfort on Mackinnon's face.

"It is a necessary process," he said. "It's the only way we are able to produce antivenom in sufficient quantities. The process itself isn't too stressful for the snake either. If you have the time, I can show you how we do it."

Mackinnon didn't really want to, but he forced himself to agree. It could help the case and move things forward.

Claude made his way over to one of the snake enclosures. Mackinnon was exceedingly glad to see that there was only a small snake inside. Claude had put on some padded gloves, and he reached inside with a clasping stick, designed to capture the snake at the base of its head. His other hand secured the slithering reptile's tail and he lifted the yellow snake out carefully.

Mackinnon took a wary step backwards.

"She's a beauty, isn't she?" Claude beamed at the snake in his hands.

Mackinnon remained silent. He didn't want to do or say anything that would distract Claude while he was holding the snake.

They made their way over to a different lab bench.

"This area is known as the milking station," Claude said and he released the tail. Sensing freedom, the snake wriggled wildly, but to Mackinnon's relief, the contraption Claude was using to hold its head stopped the snake from escaping.

Claude picked up a twenty-five millilitre container and held it up for Mackinnon to see. "See the rubber on top?"

Mackinnon moved a little closer and peered down at the container. The top of the small pot was lined with a semi-opaque sheath.

"The snake is going to bite and its fangs will pierce the rubber. The venom will be squirted inside for us to collect."

When Claude moved the container close to the snake's head, at first it seemed not to be interested in biting. Mackinnon felt himself relax. It was only a small snake and it seemed quite docile. But suddenly without warning, it pounced. Its fangs plunged through the rubber sheath. Mackinnon could see the venom trickle down into the pot.

"You see," Claude said. "It's easy."

Mackinnon, who was sweating buckets and was sure it had less to do with the increased temperature in the reptile house and more to do with the proximity of the yellow snake Claude was holding, just nodded.

"I have another question," Mackinnon said. "What do you do about antivenom?"

Claude nodded. "Sensible question. We always keep some in stock and so do the local hospitals. We haven't had to use it since I've been here, but most people handling venomous snakes would have their own supply."

Mackinnon hoped that was true. Right now, it seemed that was their best chance of catching the killer.

CHAPTER TWENTY-FOUR

AFTER HE LEFT CLAUDE AND his snakes behind, Mackinnon pulled out his phone and called DI Tyler.

"I think we are looking for a snake expert," Mackinnon said as he walked along Camden High Street in the direction of the tube station. "It seems easy enough to extract the venom if you know how to handle them."

"Right. What about the antivenom?"

"They keep it in stock and so do the local hospitals. It is a strong possibility that whoever is using this Russell's viper venom will have stocks of the relevant antivenom."

"Let's hope so," Tyler said. "Are you coming back to the station now?"

"I'm just about to get on the train. Have there been any more developments?"

"Yes," Tyler said. "An interesting one. Evie Charlesworth has found a connection. It's a tenuous one at the moment, but it's the only thing we have to link the two victims."

Mackinnon paused at the entrance to the underground station. He wanted to hear what Tyler said next and didn't want to risk losing his mobile phone signal. He leaned back against the wall as people rushed past him, heading for the escalator to take them down into the belly of London.

"Beverley Madison and Joe Griffin both went to the same school," Tyler said. "It was a while ago, class of eighty-seven, but they were both at St George's at the same time. It's our first indication that our victims may have known each other.

"We've got the tech team going over all their social media accounts, trying to find out if they've been keeping in touch. We are also combing their phone and financial records. Nothing so far, but if we continue on this line, we *might* get lucky."

Tyler drew a long breath and Mackinnon could sense what was coming.

"We might…" Mackinnon said. "But you don't think we will?"

"It is a connection but it might not be the great lead it appears to be. Brookbank has fastened onto the idea. He wants lists of past students and staff and he wants us to interview them. It's a huge task. We have to go all the way back to nineteen eighty-seven. I know Brookbank is just being thorough, but…" Tyler swallowed his words with a heavy sigh.

After a moment's pause, he said, "It's a rabbit hole, Jack. It's going to take ages, and the more time we waste on this, the more likely it is our killer will strike again."

Mackinnon could see both points of view. Right now, the school was the only link they had, and so it made sense to focus some of their resources on investigating that connection. But resources weren't unlimited, and it was clear Tyler was worried that they would overlook other potential leads if they focused solely on this.

"You know what Brookbank is like once he has got a bee in his bonnet," Tyler said. "It looks like he's going to put most of the team on this, tracking down ex-students and staff, but it's crazy. I mean, how likely is it they stayed in the same place since nineteen eighty-seven? They're going to be all over the country, some of them might be abroad."

Mackinnon looked up at the grey December sky and couldn't help agreeing with Tyler. He didn't much fancy interviewing hundreds of ex-students, surely there could be a better way to use the resources.

"Anyway," Tyler said. "I'll ask Collins to focus on any criminal records first. Hopefully that will give us a hit and save us interviewing every Tom, Dick or Harry who got within one hundred yards of the bloody school."

Mackinnon could hear the stress in Tyler's voice. He told him he'd be back at the station within half an hour and hung up. As he took the escalator down into the underground station, he couldn't help thinking that Tyler was right. This case was a rabbit hole.

* * *

Shortly after Mackinnon got back to Wood Street station, DCI Brookbank called an emergency briefing.

As DI Tyler sat scowling in the corner, obviously

unhappy with the direction the investigation was taking, Brookbank assigned everyone new actions.

"We need to focus on the link between our victims." He nodded at Mackinnon and Charlotte. "Jack and Charlotte, I want you to go to St George's Academy and talk to the headmistress there. She is…" Brookbank looked down at his notes. "Sandra Diamond. Talk to her, find out if there are any staff still at the school who were working there in nineteen eighty-seven." Brookbank shrugged. "It's a long shot, but we might get lucky."

Mackinnon nodded and then shot a look at DI Tyler who was rolling his eyes.

"With respect, sir," DC Webb said in a nervous voice. "All we've got is two victims who went to the same school. It could be a coincidence."

Brookbank stared at DC Webb, who seemed to shrink in his chair.

"It could be," Brookbank conceded. "But right now, we don't have another link, so that's where we're going to focus our energy."

"We need to make sure we don't overlook any other links," DC Collins said, and Mackinnon admired him for speaking up. "They could have shopped in the same supermarket every week, or gone to the same evening class five years ago."

Brookbank put down his sheaf of notes and steadily surveyed the room. "All right. I sense your reluctance, and to some extent, I understand it. They don't shop at the same supermarket, DC Collins. If they had, we would have discovered that when we looked at their financial records."

Collins looked down at the table and nodded.

"As for the evening class idea, sure it's a possibility, but we don't have any evidence of that. We do have evidence that they went to the same school and that is what we need to investigate. It may lead to nothing, but it's all we have right now. So is everyone on board?" Brookbank glared at everyone in the room, and Mackinnon didn't think anyone would dare disagree.

"The thing is," Tyler said from the corner of the room and everyone turned to face him. "I understand that we need to investigate this."

Mackinnon could see the 'but' coming from a mile away. The air seemed to have been sucked out of the room. It was generally accepted in the briefings that people could give opinions and be open with ideas. Sometimes that was how seemingly unsolvable cases were cracked. Even the most junior staff could have a great idea that no one else had thought of, but a high ranked officer casting doubt on the action plan of the senior investigating officer was pretty much a no-no.

Mackinnon waited with interest to see Brookbank's reaction.

Brookbank turned his thick neck and hunched his shoulders as he faced Tyler.

Tyler didn't back down. He continued, "I need Charlotte to keep working on the DWA licences and the antivenom. We can't let that go in favour of this link with St George's."

Brookbank nodded. "Absolutely. I agree one hundred percent."

Tyler looked surprised. He nodded. "Okay… Well, that's good, and I want to prioritise by having us look at students or staff with records."

"Agreed," Brookbank said and began to gather his papers together. "Okay, if everyone knows what they are doing, we'll meet again this evening," Brookbank said as he brought the meeting to a close.

Mackinnon got to his feet and filed out of the meeting room with the rest of the team. It was going to be a long day and he had to start it by going back to school.

CHAPTER TWENTY-FIVE

MACKINNON HEADED TO ST GEORGE'S Academy on his own, leaving Charlotte to track down people who had purchased antivenom over the past six months.

St George's had been built in the fifties, but had undergone some changes over the past few years. It was now an Academy, focusing on business and sports. The outside of the school was plain red brick. Mackinnon thought it was more attractive than most of the modern comprehensives he had seen.

When he had been at school, Mackinnon remembered pretty much anyone could just walk across the playground and into the school. St George's was surrounded by twelve-foot high fences, and admission was through a gate that only opened at certain times of the day.

Mackinnon rubbed his forehead, feeling a headache developing, probably due to his lack of sleep.

He pressed the buzzer beside the gate and waited until a

crackly voice came over the intercom. He had phoned ahead, so they were quick to admit him. The gate clanged shut behind him, and he walked across the empty playground towards the entrance.

He was intercepted by an efficient-looking secretary before he reached the blue double doors. The secretary introduced herself as Mrs. Rogers and escorted Mackinnon into the building.

The inside of the building was far more modern than the outside had indicated. There was a large atrium, and as he had arrived just in time for the changeover between lessons, the kids' voices echoed around the great hall and their trainers squeaked against the floor. That was something new. Trainers would never have been permitted as part of the school uniform in Mackinnon's day. The uniform at St George's consisted of dark grey trousers, for both the boys and the girls, and navy blue sweatshirts, with the school's logo embroidered on the chest.

The secretary led the way to the headmistress' office. She rapped on the door and then stood back, gesturing for Mackinnon to enter the room.

Mrs. Sandra Diamond stood up when Mackinnon entered her office. He guessed the plump, grey-haired lady must be nearing retirement.

She held out her hand to Mackinnon. "Detective, I'm Sandra Diamond the headmistress of St George's. How can I help?"

Mackinnon sat in one of the chairs in front of her desk. From the doorway, the secretary asked if they would like some coffee. Mackinnon said he would. He was going to need a lot of coffee to get through the day.

"Thank you for seeing me at such short notice," Mackinnon said. "I know you must be very busy."

"Not at all," Mrs. Diamond said. "I will be quite happy to help in any way I can."

"I'm sure you've heard on the news about the unusual murders in the city."

Mrs. Diamond nodded. "Yes, I did see that last night. We usually have the news on in the background while we eat our dinner. Do you somehow think it is related to the school?"

"We are just checking into the victims' backgrounds," Mackinnon said, eager to reassure her. "It just so happens that the victims were students here in the past."

Mrs. Diamond's forehead crinkled as she raised her eyebrows. "Really? I didn't recognise the names."

"Well, the students attended the school some time ago. They would have started at St George's in nineteen eighty-seven."

"I was here then," Mrs. Diamond said. "This is the only school I've worked at. I completed my training at a school in North London, but I came here straight after I graduated." Mrs. Diamond shook her head. "I can't say I recognised them as St. George's students when I heard the news. Remind me again, what were their names?"

"Beverley Madison and Joe Griffin," Mackinnon said.

"I'm sorry. They don't ring any bells. I can have a look through the records for you, though." She pushed back her chair from the desk. "I'm afraid we will have to look through the paper records and deal with the old filing system. You see, we didn't have computerised records in the eighties. We are supposed to be moving everything over to the computer, but these things do take time."

"Of course," Mackinnon said. "I'm glad to hear you have paper records."

"We should be able to access them quite quickly. They're stored next door in the secretary's office. If you'll excuse me, I will ask Mrs. Rogers if she can pick them out for us."

At that moment, the secretary, Mrs. Rogers, brought in a tray containing two steaming cups of coffee. Mackinnon took a cup gratefully, breathing in one of his favourite smells in the world. It may not have pleased a coffee connoisseur, but it was hot and it contained caffeine and that was all Mackinnon cared about.

Mrs. Diamond asked the secretary to find the files and then turned back to Mackinnon. "Isn't it unusual that both victims were students of this school? Do you think the school could be involved?"

"It's something we're looking into," Mackinnon said, unwilling to commit himself further. "We need to find out everything we can about each of the victims, no matter how insignificant it may seem."

Mackinnon took a sip of his coffee. "Both Beverley and Joe would have been here between the years of nineteen eighty-seven and nineteen ninety-one. Did anything significant happen during those years?"

"Like what?" Mrs. Diamond asked.

That wasn't an easy question to answer. He didn't know what they were looking for.

"Did anything happen in the school's history? Any incidents, good or bad? Bullying? Perhaps the school had some trouble with a member of staff?"

"Goodness," Mrs. Diamond said. "Now you are putting me on the spot." She put her fingertips against her temples and gazed down at her desk as if she was concentrating.

"I do remember something happening in the early nineties. It was rather upsetting. A boy hanged himself. A terribly sad situation," she said gazing over at the window and then back to Mackinnon. "If I recall correctly, it was put down to pressure over exam results. It was a difficult year for us. We lost another student that same year. It was an accident — an asthma attack."

"What year was that? Do you remember?" Mackinnon asked.

"I would have to check the records to be sure, but I think it was probably ninety-one or ninety-two," Mrs. Diamond said. She picked up her coffee cup as the secretary came back into the room and laid a collection of files down on her desk.

"Here they are. They weren't too difficult to find after all," the secretary said, pushing her glasses back on the bridge of her nose. "Sometimes the old ways are the best. You don't get paper files crashing or getting infected with viruses, do you?"

"Thank you," Mrs. Diamond said, reaching for one of the files. "I know you prefer the more traditional methods but we need to get these records onto the computer system as soon as possible."

The secretary glared at Mackinnon as if he was personally responsible for upsetting her filing system.

"Is that all for now?"

"Yes, thank you, Mrs. Rogers." Mrs. Diamond flicked through the first file. "Ah, yes. I do remember Joe Griffin.

Of course I do. He was the head of the school rugby team, very sporty." She flicked through a few more pages of the records and then said, "Yes, he did the school proud. I always thought he might go on and compete internationally. He didn't I suppose?" Mrs. Diamond looked at Mackinnon hopefully.

Mackinnon shook his head. "After he left school, he joined the Navy for two years and then changed career paths. He became a personal trainer."

Mrs. Diamond plucked the other file from her desk and flipped through it. "Beverley Madison..." She murmured the name as she held up the first page of the file and turned it around for Mackinnon to see. It was a picture of Beverley taken while she'd been a pupil at St George's. Mackinnon guessed she must have been around fourteen when the photograph was taken. She had blonde bobbed hair and a sunny smile.

"I'm afraid I can't remember Beverley," she said. "I hate to admit it, but there have been so many you see."

"Of course," Mackinnon said. "You can't be expected to remember every single student."

Mrs. Diamond shook her head. "No, and of course when Joe and Beverley were here I was a science teacher. I had to take a lot of classes, and I'm afraid if a student wasn't terribly behaved or exceptionally bright, they didn't get a great deal of my attention. It's an unfortunate situation, but sadly the truth in education these days. I read something about her in the paper this morning. Wasn't she quite a high flyer?"

Mackinnon nodded. "Beverley had done very well for herself. She was a literary agent and a very successful one."

Mrs. Diamond nodded. "Yes, I read that she represented Jacob Jansen. You know, I am quite a fan of his work." She gave a coy smile and put Beverley's file down on her desk with a sigh. "It's funny. You think you can tell which of the students will go on and make a success of their lives, but nine times out of ten, I get it wrong."

"Were Beverley and Joe friends? Did they hang around in the same group?" Mackinnon asked. "I'm looking for things they may have had in common."

Mrs. Diamond gave him an apologetic look. "It's such a long time ago. I'm afraid the school records wouldn't tell me if they were friends or if they spent time together. I don't even have records of which students were in the same classes. The only thing I can tell you from looking at these files is that they weren't in the same form group. But that doesn't mean they didn't have certain subjects together. Or whether they were friends out of school."

Mackinnon nodded. They didn't seem to be having much luck coming up with connections between Joe Griffin and Beverley Madison. He finished up with a few more questions and then thanked Mrs. Diamond for his coffee and prepared to leave.

Mrs. Diamond shuffled the files together in a neat pile on her desk. She shivered.

"I do hope there isn't a connection with the school," Mrs. Diamond said. "It gives me the creeps just thinking about it."

CHAPTER TWENTY-SIX

AS SOON AS HE LEFT the school, Mackinnon pulled out his mobile phone and dialled Tyler's number.

"Go on," Tyler said. "Give me the worst of it."

"I didn't have much luck," Mackinnon said. "The only thing that could be of interest was a male pupil who hung himself in either nineteen ninety-one or ninety-two. It could coincide with the time period that Joe and Beverley attended St George's. Another kid died of an asthma attack the same year. Sandra Diamond is going to check the records and get back to me."

"Nothing else?" Tyler sounded despondent.

"I'm afraid not. She couldn't remember any of the other children they hung around with or even tell me whether they were in the same classes for different subjects. For all we know, they may have had nothing to do with each other while they were at the school."

Tyler exhaled. "Great. I knew it. We're wasting our time."

"Have we had any luck on the antivenom front?" Mackinnon asked, thinking of the work Charlotte was doing back at the station.

Tyler huffed out a breath that was half a laugh and half a sigh. "Not bloody likely. You were at the briefing. You heard Brookbank tell me he was happy for Charlotte to keep on digging and find out who had ordered antivenom in the last six months."

"Yes, I heard him say that. Did he change his mind?"

"You could say that. For the last hour, she's been checking the DWA licences against a list of ex-students and faculty members from St George's. Honestly, it's a complete waste of time."

"Then tell Brookbank."

"I've tried that," Tyler said. Mackinnon could tell he was speaking through gritted teeth. "Anyway, there's no point in me moaning about it. It isn't going to get me anywhere, is it? I'll just have to work my way through this list and get this stuff out of the way as quickly as possible so we can focus on other possible leads."

When Mackinnon got back to the station, Tyler miserably handed him a stack of paper. "This is only *part* of the list," he said. "We've got contact details and last known addresses. We need to ring every single one of them and try to unearth any connections."

Mackinnon groaned. It was going to be a long afternoon.

* * *

The day had dragged on and on, and Tyler couldn't wait to see the back of it. He'd spent most of the afternoon going through information gathered by the teams of uniforms he'd sent out to interview people who had attended the school.

Brookbank was back in the incident room, overseeing the investigation, and Tyler had decided to call it a night. He had worked late last night and was feeling grumpy and irritable. It would only get worse if he didn't get any sleep.

He took a couple of files with him, planning to make some house calls himself on the way home and make some headway. He tucked a wedge of papers under his arm, scooped up his keys and headed out into the car park.

He threw the paperwork onto the passenger seat and then started the car, turning the heaters on full blast.

He pulled the car out of the car park and on to Love Lane. At the junction, he had to slow the car for a group of after-work revellers who were weaving across the road, wearing stupid Santa hats.

Tyler cursed them under his breath and switched the radio on. As an impossibly cheerful Christmas song blasted out of the speakers, he quickly switched it back off again. He wasn't feeling Christmassy at all.

Since his wife had left last year, there never seemed much point in rushing home. Tonight it would be just him and a microwave meal for one.

Most of the other officers had homes to go to with families waiting for them, wanting to spend time with them.

Tyler typed the first address into the satnav on his dashboard and followed the directions through the London streets.

The addresses he'd picked out for tonight were all in Whitechapel. The first address was on Bakers Lane. He had planned to make a serious dent in the list tonight. He knew what questions to ask and would be in and out of each address within a couple of minutes.

But Tyler's high hopes faded when he found there was no one home at the first property. On the way back to the car, he managed to plunge his feet into an icy puddle beside the kerb. He stared down at his sopping wet feet. *Could this day get any worse?*

He swore under his breath and stalked back to the car, grabbing the list from the passenger seat. The next address was only around the corner, so he decided to leave the car where it was, seeing as he had found a parking space, which were as rare as hens' teeth around here.

He walked around into the next street, his right foot squelching noisily in his shoe.

The next name on his list was Troy Scott, who lived in a ground floor flat. Tyler smiled when he saw that the light was on in the hallway.

At least this one wouldn't be a complete waste of time.

He rang the doorbell and waited, but after thirty seconds, he grew impatient and rapped on the wood-panelled door.

Still no answer.

He could see the outline of a Christmas tree through the net curtains. The coloured lights were flashing on and off in a garish display.

Tyler leaned against the railing and peered through a gap in the curtain into the bay windows.

He could see someone inside.

A man was sitting in front of his computer, ignoring him.

Tyler hammered on the door as loudly as he could, drawing the attention of Troy Scott's neighbour in the flat above him. He gave the woman a thumbs up sign. She scowled at him and closed her curtains, but Tyler had achieved his aim. The man sitting at the computer had finally noticed him.

Tyler stamped his freezing cold feet, trying to keep warm as he waited for the door to open.

CHAPTER TWENTY-SEVEN

I'D BEEN ONLY SECONDS AWAY from making my move when I heard the doorbell. The panic threatened to overwhelm me at first, and I stood in the hallway with my heart thudding in my chest. It took a few seconds for me to realise I needed to find a hiding place. Fast.

I quickly ducked inside the cupboard under the stairs. It was cramped and filled with junk. I could only hope that whoever was at the door wouldn't stay long.

My hands were shaking uncontrollably as I attempted to put the cap back on the needle. The door to the cupboard was only slightly ajar, letting in a thin sliver of light. It was so dark I knew I could easily make a mistake and stab my finger. Then it would all be over.

Finally, I managed to replace the cap, and I let out a shaky relieved breath. I set the syringe on the floor next to a tatty old pair of trainers and crouched down next to a half-inflated football and a cricket bat.

The doorbell rang again.

Go away, I thought. He can't hear you.

When I had snuck in through the back door, I had seen Troy Scott sitting at the computer. He had headphones covering his ears and was moving his head in time to whatever music was playing. I'd taken that as a sign that things were going to go smoothly. I had imagined myself walking up behind him quietly, puncturing his skin with the syringe at the very last moment.

It should have been perfect. It would have been if some idiot wasn't ringing the doorbell.

I was starting to get a cramp in my leg and got up from my crouched position, trying to flex my foot without making any noise. Whoever it was would give up soon, and I willed myself to relax.

After a few seconds of silence, I thought the person at the door had gone away, but I wasn't so lucky. The sound of loud hammering on the door made me flinch back into the shadows.

I heard the wheels of Troy Scott's chair moving against the hardwood floor as he finally noticed there was somebody to see him.

I held my breath as he walked straight past my hiding place towards the front door.

I should have pulled the cupboard door closed properly behind me, but I couldn't do anything about it now without him noticing.

I heard the rattle as he opened his front door, and then I heard a voice say, "Are you Troy Scott?"

There was something about the man's voice that set my

nerves on edge. A terrifying feeling of dread welled up inside me. I didn't understand why, but somehow I knew he was a threat.

"Yes," Troy Scott said, his voice betraying his irritation. "What do you want? If you are selling something, I am not interested. I'm trying to work, and you have interrupted me in the middle of a job."

"I'm not selling anything," the man at the door replied. "I've come to ask you a few questions. I'm DI Tyler, City of London police."

My breath froze in my chest.

Police.

What was he doing here?

It couldn't be about me. It was too early. There was no way they could have figured it all out yet.

I tried to move closer and peer out of the small gap, but I couldn't see either of them from my hiding place.

I wrapped my arms around my midsection, trying to control my trembling. It had to be a coincidence. Yes, that was it. He was probably here about a stolen bike or a lost mobile phone... But even as I tried to reassure myself, I knew deep down there was no way a detective inspector would be here about a lost mobile phone.

Troy let him inside, and as they both moved down the hallway I got a glimpse of the detective inspector. I bit down on the inside of my mouth so hard I tasted blood.

I recognised him.

I'd seen him outside the hotel.

He was medium height, perhaps five-foot nine at a guess, and he was of slim build. He looked about warily as he entered the hallway. His eyes skimmed across the cupboard door, where I was hiding, and I could have sworn he looked straight at me.

"I've just got a few questions for you," DI Tyler said. "Can you confirm that you attended St. George's School from nineteen eighty-seven to nineteen ninety-two?"

They walked into the sitting room. From my position, I could just see the detective as he sat down on the sofa, but I couldn't see Troy.

"Yeah, that's right. Do we have to do this now? I'm in the middle of a project. I have to make tonight's deadline otherwise I'll let my client down." Troy's voice sounded bored.

"It won't take long." The detective pulled out a notebook and pen. "You have probably heard about it in the news. There have been two murders recently—"

"All that stuff about The Charmer?" Troy interrupted with a definite mocking tone. I could picture his smirking face.

"The victims went to St George's."

I raised my hand to my mouth.

I could just imagine Troy's relaxed shrug as he said, "Well, I would guess a lot of people went to that school over the years."

"Yes, you're right, of course," the detective said. "But I was wondering if you remembered anything about your time at school that could be relevant. Perhaps something that only seems significant now in light of recent events?"

"Not really," Troy said. "What sort of thing do you mean?"

The detective stared in Troy's direction, and I must have imagined it, but I was sure that I could see dislike on his face.

"What is it you do for a living, sir?"

"I am a website designer, and I was in the middle of working on one right now for a very important client actually, so if that is all, I'd like to get back to it."

"No, Mr. Scott, that isn't all," the detective said, and he stood up so suddenly I felt sure he was going to rush into the hallway and tell me the game was up.

But he didn't.

He had spotted something in the corner of the sitting room and jabbed a finger in its direction. "What the hell is that?" he demanded.

"What?" Troy Scott said. "Oh, you mean my snake?"

I exhaled slowly and realised I'd been holding my breath. The detective had seen the corn snake that Troy kept in a tank in the corner of his living room.

"It's harmless," Troy said. "I've kept them ever since I was a boy."

For a moment, the detective said nothing. I could almost hear the cogs turning in his brain. My plan for tonight was about to change drastically.

I glanced around the small cupboard for something that I could use as a weapon. My fingers closed around the solid handle of the cricket bat. I lifted it silently. It would have to do.

"Right," the detective said, nodding to himself and sitting back on the sofa. He flipped open his notepad and wrote something down. "There was an incident at the school back in nineteen ninety-one. A boy hanged himself. Can you tell me anything about that?"

"Kevin," Troy said. "Yeah, I remember that. It was Kevin Cooper. He was in the same year as me. I'm not sure what I can tell you about him. It was just before the exams, and I guess he decided it was all a bit too much."

The detective scribbled something else on his notepad. I chewed on my lip and couldn't help wondering what he was making a note of.

"Did anything else out of the ordinary happen that year?"

"No, not that I remember," Troy said.

My hand tightened around the handle of the cricket bat.

"Okay," the detective said, getting to his feet again. "That's all the questions I have for you for now."

He walked back out into the hallway, raking his hand through his grey hair, and Troy followed him.

At the last moment, the detective turned around and said, "Oh, yes, there was one more thing I wanted to ask you about. Were you aware of any bullying at the school?"

I could see them both clearly now, and I saw the flash of hesitation pass over Troy Scott's face. So did the detective.

"It's nothing to worry about. We all did things when we were kids, didn't we?" The detective smiled and shrugged. "Sometimes things can go a bit too far. But you can tell me. You're not going to get in any trouble for something you did back then."

"Well," Troy said hesitantly, looking uncomfortable.

He was going to tell him something. I couldn't let that happen.

"I wasn't really involved. It wasn't my fault." His voice cracked. "You see, there was…"

But Troy Scott never managed to finish his sentence. I slipped out of the cupboard, raised the cricket bat above my head and smashed it down hard against the detective's skull.

CHAPTER TWENTY-EIGHT

MY HEART WAS RACING, AND my hands were so sweaty that the cricket bat slid from my fingers and dropped to the floor.

I stared at the detective sprawled out at my feet.

No. No. No. That wasn't supposed to happen. It wasn't part of the plan.

It wasn't my fault. I didn't want to do it, but I had to. Troy Scott had been about to ruin everything.

I'd been so dazed by what I had done, I'd momentarily forgotten why I'd come here.

I blinked and jerked my head around to see Troy Scott staring at me with his mouth open.

Corn snake boy was too dumb to move. I would have thought that in a situation like this self-preservation would have kicked in and he would have taken the opportunity to run.

Perhaps he was in shock.

He didn't move at all as I walked back to the cupboard, scooped up the syringe and began to approach him.

"Who the hell are you?" Troy demanded, finally finding his voice as I closed the distance between us.

So he didn't recognise me. I had expected as much.

He should have been less concerned with who I was and more concerned with what I was about to do.

I slid the cap from the syringe, and with one quick movement I stabbed the needle in his thigh, pushing down the plunger before he even had a chance to react.

He reared away from me, gripping his leg.

"What are you doing? What on earth was that?" He stumbled backwards.

He fired questions at me. His anger, confusion and panic were all reflected in his face.

He carried on shouting his questions, but I didn't answer.

Watching someone who is about to die is fascinating. You would think they would do something important or profound, but they don't.

They don't make the most of the minutes they have left. They do stupid things like ask the same question over and over again.

"He was a policeman! There will be more of them here any time now." He grabbed an ornamental poker from beside the fireplace and waved it around. "You're crazy. You stabbed me and you have killed a policeman."

I took a step towards him, and he slashed the air with the poker. "Keep away from me." His voice was high-pitched and shaky.

"Look at him," Troy screamed. "Look at what you have done."

I stared down at the detective's prone body and swallowed hard. The grey hair on the back of his head was dark with blood. I turned away quickly. I didn't want to see that.

Troy made a grab for the landline telephone, but I leaned down and unplugged the cable from the wall.

He stared at me in disbelief. His lower lip wobbled as if he couldn't believe I had done something so cruel. I didn't know why it was so much of a shock to him. After all, I'd just bashed someone over the head with a cricket bat and stabbed him with a needle. Fear made some people illogical.

For a few seconds he did nothing except stare at me, searching for answers.

The hand Troy was using to grip the poker was trembling. He used the back of his left hand to wipe the sweat from his forehead.

It wouldn't be long now.

He stumbled back over to his computer workstation, grabbing his mobile phone off the desk. He slumped against the wall as his fingers desperately pressed the keys.

I should have stopped him, but I didn't.

I glanced back at the detective's body. The ambulance and police Troy was calling for would arrive too late for him, but I hoped they wouldn't be too late for the detective.

I slid the folded obituary notice from the pocket of my coat and pinned it to the corkboard above the computer.

Troy was gripped with a spasm of pain and moaned as he bent double. I stayed to watch until he was curled up in a foetal position on the hardwood floor.

Then I stepped over the detective's body as I left Troy's apartment.

CHAPTER TWENTY-NINE

MACKINNON GOT BACK TO HIS house on Woodstock Road in Oxford just before eight pm. He still had mountains of work to do, but he had promised Katy that they would sit down over dinner and discuss her problems at school. And he took that promise seriously.

When he let himself in the front door, the smell of garlic hit him, and he could hear the clatter of pans and utensils coming from the kitchen.

He called out and Chloe poked her head around the kitchen door. She grinned and then walked towards him, pulling him into a hug as he was still shrugging off his coat.

"I'm glad you made it home," Chloe said. "I thought you might have to call and cancel."

Mackinnon kissed her on the forehead and hung his coat on the hook by the door. "It's pretty frantic at the moment, but I didn't want to let Katy down."

Chloe smiled. "We've got a stir-fry for dinner. It's almost ready."

"Lovely." Mackinnon followed Chloe into the kitchen, and a moment later, there was the sound of furious footsteps on the stairs as Katy raced down from her bedroom.

She grinned widely at Mackinnon, before remembering she didn't want to show quite how glad she was to see him. Her grin turned to a frown.

"Can you set the table please, Katy?" Chloe asked as she picked up a spatula and began to add prawns to the stir-fry.

Katy opened the drawer and began to select the knives and forks.

"No Sarah tonight?" Mackinnon opened a cupboard and took out two wine glasses.

"No. She's gone out again."

Sarah had been attending Kingston University for the past few months, and although she was supposed to be home for the Christmas holidays, they hadn't seen much of her yet.

"Is she still talking about going to New Zealand?" Mackinnon asked.

A few weeks ago Sarah had spoken to her father who lived in New Zealand, and he had promised to pay for her flight out to see him this Christmas. Unfortunately, he didn't seem to be following through on his promise, and neither Chloe nor Sarah could get in touch with him.

"Yes, she is still insisting she is going to spend Christmas there. I know she hasn't heard from him." Chloe lowered her voice so that Katy, who was setting the table in the dining room, wouldn't hear her. "In all likelihood, he has changed his mind or he has spoken to his wife, and *she* doesn't want Sarah there at Christmas." Chloe shrugged. "I've tried talking to her, trying to prepare her for the fact that he probably won't come through with the ticket, but I just end up sounding like the bad guy."

Mackinnon poured two glasses of red wine.

"I guess we just have to wait and see. Maybe he will do the right thing this time."

Chloe raised an eyebrow but said nothing.

Mackinnon walked into the dining room to ask Katy what she wanted to drink with dinner.

"Just water, thanks." Then she added in a lowered voice, "You *are* going to stick up for me, right?"

"We're both on your side," Mackinnon said. "We only want what is best for you."

Katy frowned and straightened a fork on the table. "Yeah, right."

Before long, they were gathered around the table tucking in to the prawn stir-fry. Mackinnon hoped that by treating Katy like an adult she would open up and explain why she wanted to leave her school.

"I realise you haven't been happy there," Chloe said. "But you only have two more years there. Once you have done your GCSEs…"

Katy put down her fork. "I couldn't stand being there for another two days. There's no way I could do it for two years!"

"Why don't you tell us what it is about the school that you don't like?" Mackinnon prompted.

Katy looked down at her plate and fiddled with the

edge of the tablecloth. "There's a group of girls who gang up on me."

"If you are being bullied we can speak to the teachers and put a stop to it."

Katy gave her mother a scornful look. "The teachers are just as bad. They never listen to me, and if you go and talk to them, you will only make things worse."

Mackinnon took another bite of his stir-fry and let Chloe ask the questions. He didn't want Katy to feel like they were ganging up on her.

"What would you do if this were a job?" Chloe asked. "You can't just run away from every problem. We need to try and find a solution."

"If it was a job I could quit and get another one. I wouldn't be forced to go to that awful place every day. I've told you why I wanted to leave. You promised you would listen to me."

She pushed her chair back from the table and looked at Mackinnon accusingly. "You *said* you would listen."

She got up from the table, and leaving her half eaten stir-fry on her plate, she fled the dining room.

Chloe called after her. "Come back here. You don't just run off like that, you *ask* to leave the table…"

But Katy didn't return.

Chloe sighed then put her head in her hands.

"I think…" Mackinnon started to say.

Chloe put her hand up. "All right. I know. You're going to say you think we should take her out of the school and let her go to a different one." She looked up at Mackinnon. "But, Jack, this is her *future*. The school is excellent. How am

I going to find another school with the same reputation in the middle of the school year?

"I hate the thought of her being bullied, Jack. I'd love to go in there and sort those girls out myself, but I can't."

Mackinnon wasn't going to argue the point. He knew that the decision was Chloe's, and it wasn't an easy one.

CHAPTER THIRTY

THE FOLLOWING MORNING, KATY STILL didn't want to go to school. Chloe had to read her the riot act just to get her out of bed, and a tearful Katy had refused to eat anything for breakfast. She sat at the kitchen counter looking at them both reproachfully.

Mackinnon managed to polish off a couple of slices of toast and a cup of coffee. He was just loading the dishwasher when his phone rang. The caller ID told him it was Charlotte.

"I'll be in at about nine thirty," Mackinnon said. "I'm travelling in from Oxford today."

"Have you heard about last night? About what happened to Tyler?" Charlotte asked without preamble.

Mackinnon closed the dishwasher door with a click. "What happened?"

As he walked towards the door and reached for his coat

he heard Charlotte take a shaky breath on the other end of the phone.

"What is it?"

"I'm at the scene now," Charlotte said. "It's awful, Jack. We're not quite sure what happened, but we think Tyler must have gone out last night, calling at some of the addresses of the ex-students. He was attacked. He was hit over the head."

"Christ. Is he all right now?"

"He's still unconscious. He is in intensive care at the moment. It doesn't look good."

Mackinnon felt a cold shiver of dread run through his body and the beginnings of heartburn building in the centre of his chest. He wished he hadn't eaten that toast.

He shrugged on his coat and stepped out of the house, closing the front door behind him.

"How the hell did it happen?"

"That's not the worst of it," Charlotte said. "He was found in a flat belonging to a man called Troy Scott, who was a student at St George's Academy at the same time as Beverley Madison and Joe Griffin. Troy Scott was murdered using the same venom and Tyler was left for dead.

"They were found because Troy Scott was supposed to be designing a website for a client, and when Troy didn't deliver by the deadline, the client tried to reach him at home. He didn't get an answer, but looking through the letterbox he saw Tyler on the floor in the hallway."

"Tyler wasn't injected with the venom?"

"No, thank God."

After a brief period of silence, Charlotte said, "It's just

awful. I don't understand why he didn't tell anyone where he was going. It's totally against protocol."

Mackinnon didn't say so, but he knew it wasn't the first time Tyler had gone against the rules.

"I know we've seen some horrific things," Charlotte said. "But they used a cricket bat on him, Jack. He could have been lying there alone for hours."

"I'll be there as soon as I can," Mackinnon said.

* * *

When Mackinnon arrived at the ground floor flat where Tyler had been attacked, he turned round in the hallway, slowly surveying the scene. Troy Scott's body had already been removed. DI Tyler had been found unconscious close to the front door. Mackinnon looked down at the blood on the beige rug marked by a yellow evidence label.

Charlotte appeared at the end of the hallway and made her way towards Mackinnon, carefully sticking to the area marked out by the crime scene manager.

"Any news on Tyler?" Mackinnon asked.

"Cerebral swelling apparently. They're not sure when he'll wake up…" Charlotte rubbed the spot between her eyebrows. "The doctors are not even sure *if* he'll wake up."

"Christ."

Charlotte took a deep breath, steadying herself. "Right, I better talk you through it. Tyler was found here." She pointed to the bloodstained carpet. "Troy Scott was working on a project for a client, and when he didn't deliver, the client came around to find out why. He'd employed Troy Scott to set up a website on short notice. He was really annoyed when he thought he'd been let down, so he came around to have it out with Troy and find out why he wasn't answering his phone. He could see that the lights were on but nobody answered the door. He peered through the letterbox because he thought Troy was just trying to avoid him, but when he did, he saw Tyler's body lying just here at the entrance to the hallway."

Charlotte bit down on her lip as she looked down at the spot where Tyler had fallen, focusing on the area of dark red blood.

"The blood has soaked into the carpet as you can see," Charlotte continued. "We know that the intruder hit Tyler with a cricket bat. There are blood smears on the flat surface of the bat. It's being analysed, so hopefully we will get some prints off it." Charlotte stepped forward, moving through the doorway into the living room. "This is where Troy Scott was found. His computer workstation is over there, and his body was found just in front of it. His mobile phone was right next to him, perhaps he was trying to dial for help, but there was no outgoing call registered."

"The venom may have overpowered him before he could make the call."

Charlotte nodded and her gaze swept to the other corner of the room. Mackinnon followed her line of sight.

There was a small glass tank containing stones and some foliage. In the corner of the tank, curled up, was a light yellow snake.

"So Troy Scott kept snakes. Interesting."

"He only had one, and it's a corn snake, nonvenomous. They are popular snakes to keep as pets apparently. Troy Scott kept the details of his purchase from a reptile specialist in Bristol and the vet he used. We've spoken to the vet who has known Troy Scott for a number of years. He told us Troy has kept snakes for over a decade, but never venomous species."

"And no other snakes were found on the property?"

"No," Charlotte said. "The place has been thoroughly searched and this is the only snake. There is no evidence that he ever kept venomous snakes here."

"So we are working on the theory that Troy Scott didn't attack Tyler himself? We are assuming a third person was here last night?"

"That's the current theory," Charlotte said. "It looks like Tyler was attacked from behind, but it's not clear how the intruder managed to overpower Troy Scott as well and why he didn't run for help."

Mackinnon nodded. "What's really interesting is that the killer used the cricket bat on Tyler."

Charlotte frowned. "Why is that interesting?"

"Well, if they were just trying to kill as many people as possible then why not inject Tyler with the venom. Why hit him over the head? They used the venom on Troy Scott, Beverley Madison and Joe Griffin, all members of St. George's Academy. The killer is selective. There's got to be a reason he chose those victims."

"Unfortunately for us we don't know what the reason is." Charlotte glanced at her watch. "Brookbank is holding a briefing at ten. We had better get back to the station. I'm in charge of coordinating the door-to-door enquiries, but I promised I'd get back for the briefing."

"Do you think Tyler had stumbled onto something or is

this just a coincidence? Was he in the wrong place at the wrong time?"

Charlotte shrugged as she followed Mackinnon outside. "It's difficult to know for sure."

The air was clear and cold, and their breath appeared in small white clouds in front of them as they walked along the street.

"Did he write anything down?" Mackinnon asked. "If he came here to interview Troy Scott, he would have made notes."

Tyler was old school. He still used a notepad and pen and said he couldn't get to grips working with a tablet.

"This is Tyler we're talking about," Charlotte said. "He's not known for writing everything down. He always told me writing notes stopped him listening properly."

Mackinnon smiled. That sounded like typical DI Tyler.

"He did write something though."

"What?"

"He wrote the words 'hiding something.'"

CHAPTER THIRTY-ONE

AFTER THE ATTACK ON TYLER, Charlotte had been given the job of coordinating the uniform door-to-door search of the surrounding properties so she had to leave Evie Charlesworth in charge of cross-checking the antivenom suppliers with a list of past students and staff of St George's Academy.

As soon as Charlotte got back to the station, she checked in with Evie.

"Have you had any luck?"

Evie smiled and handed her a stack of printed sheets. "Yes, we've got a name."

Charlotte listened carefully as Evie filled her in and then followed everyone else into the briefing room. She caught sight of Collins and slipped down into the seat beside him.

"Has there been any more news on Tyler's condition?" Charlotte asked.

Collins shook his head. "No change. He is still in an

induced coma, and they won't bring him out of it until the swelling goes down. It could be some time."

The mood in the meeting room was subdued. Everyone was talking in whispers as they waited for the briefing to start, and when DCI Brookbank walked into the room, everyone fell silent.

The DCI's cheeks were redder than usual and his neck had practically disappeared between his broad shoulders. He stomped his way to the front of the room, coming to a stop by the head of the table. He leant forward, resting his palms on the flat surface. He didn't bother to sit down.

"We are going to catch whoever did this," he said. "We will go through every shred of evidence with a fine-tooth comb until we catch whoever did this to one of our own. Is that understood?"

There were murmurs of consent and a row of nodding heads from the officers sitting around the table.

"DC Webb," Brookbank barked. "Where are we on the obituaries?"

DC Webb looked flustered and startled at having been called on first. "Ah, yes," he said, uncrossing his legs and shuffling through his paperwork. "I've managed to narrow things down a bit. The obituaries were posted in a weekend paper which is local to East London. Unfortunately, when I phoned them this morning they weren't keen to give out the name of the person who had purchased these obituary notices."

"We will have the warrant soon," Brookbank said. "Then it won't be a problem."

Brookbank shifted his dark blue eyes to Collins. "What have you got to report, Collins?"

"I've been going through the list of ex-students and faculty members. I've found that a few of the old students have records, mainly for minor things — shoplifting, drunk driving and a couple of domestic disturbances. But I haven't found anything that would lead me to believe one of them is our potential killer."

Brookbank nodded. "What about the family of the hanged boy? Any indication that he was bullied? Perhaps family members out for revenge?"

"I've looked at his immediate family. His parents and both brothers emigrated to Australia in nineteen ninety-five for a fresh start. Although there are still friends and extended family in the area."

Brookbank scowled. "Right. Follow it up."

Eventually he shifted his attention to Charlotte. "Where are we regarding the antivenom orders?"

"I've had Evie helping me with this," Charlotte said. "We've compared names on the dangerous wild animals licence list with people who have purchased antivenom in the last year. Then we looked for any matches with our list of ex-pupils from St George's." Charlotte took a breath, then picked up a biro from the table and circled the name on the printed sheets in front of her. "We've got a name."

Brookbank looked up and the energy in the room seemed to shift.

"His name is Lloyd Hughes. He went to the same school as Beverley Madison, Joe Griffin and Troy Scott. He had a dangerous wild animals licence five years ago, and he purchased a stock of antivenom just six months ago."

Brookbank's face spread into a cold smile. "Excellent work," he said. "That's our link. Bring him in."

* * *

Mackinnon stared angrily at his computer screen, frustrated beyond belief. Every thirty seconds, his eyes flickered to the clock on the wall. Charlotte had gone to Lloyd Hughes' address with the response team, but DCI Brookbank wanted him to stay at the station and look into Lloyd Hughes' background.

He wondered what was happening now. Surely they must have arrived at the scene already. Was Lloyd Hughes there? Or did he operate out of another address? The address registered with the DVLA indicated that he was still living with his mother. But it was possible that Lloyd Hughes had another address, one that wasn't on the public record. Maybe he stayed with a girlfriend or shared with a friend.

It wouldn't be long before Charlotte reported back, but the wait was killing him. The minutes seemed to drag by as he tried to focus on the computer screen. He knew as well as anybody that this part of the job was just as important as being there for the raids and the takedowns. It was the behind-the-scenes painstaking research and combing through all the details that meant the CPS would be able to successfully prosecute. He knew all that, but he still hated being the one left behind at the station.

From his seat in the incident room, Mackinnon could see directly into Tyler's office. DCI Brookbank was in there. His back was to Mackinnon as he looked through DI Tyler's notes and his daybook, trying to piece together what had happened to Tyler last night. They still had no idea why Tyler had visited Troy Scott last night.

Troy Scott had been on the list of people to be questioned, but it was against procedure for Tyler to go alone.

Mackinnon knew better than anyone that Tyler wasn't exactly a stickler when it came to procedure. He liked to operate outside the rules sometimes, but he was a good officer and wouldn't have put himself at risk. He found it hard to believe that if Tyler had stumbled across some new information he would have just gone around to see Troy Scott without telling anyone.

Only this morning, Charlotte had told him that Tyler had been separated from his wife for the past six months. Mackinnon had had no idea. Tyler wasn't exactly the sharing type. He had been looking tired lately, like things had been grinding him down, and Mackinnon regretted not reaching out and offering him a little bit of support.

Mackinnon's phone rang and he snatched it up from the desk. Chloe's name flashed on the screen, and he pressed the green button to answer the call.

"What's wrong?" he asked. Chloe didn't often call him during the day. She worked full-time at one of the Oxford colleges and her job kept her frantically busy. She wasn't the type to call him during office hours just for a chat, so her phone call in the middle of the morning worried him.

"I just had a call from Katy's school." She sounded worried.

"Is she ill?"

"No, but she's been sent home."

A flash of anger ran through Mackinnon. His first thought was that the girls who had been ganging up on Katy were involved and the situation had developed into physical bullying.

"Did they hurt her? Is she all right?"

"It's not that," Chloe said. Her voice sounded stressed. "Katy has been sent home from school for bad behaviour."

"Bad behaviour? Katy?" That didn't sound right at all. She was the amiable one, the hard-working one. She never caused any trouble and was the complete opposite of her sister, Sarah.

"What is she supposed to have done?"

"The headmistress phoned me. She said she didn't want to get into it over the phone, but she indicated that Katy had caused harm to another student. To be honest, I was so shocked when she called, I didn't really ask the right questions. I'm just about to leave work now and go and pick her up."

"Right," Mackinnon said, raking a hand through his hair. "Is there anything you need me to do?"

"The headmistress wants me to go in tomorrow morning for a meeting and discuss Katy's situation. Can you come? I think it would really help if we put on a united front and persuade her that Katy's got a stable home life and supportive parents. Whatever mess she's gotten into I don't want this to be on her school record, Jack."

Mackinnon leaned back in his chair. This couldn't have come at a worse time. With Tyler in the hospital, the investigation was severely short-handed, and they were so close to an arrest. But of course he couldn't say no.

"What time is the meeting? I'll make sure I'm there."

CHAPTER THIRTY-TWO

I DETESTED GOING TO VISIT my mother. I never thought I would feel like that, and I hated the care home for making me dread the visits. I could never relax. They were always watching. They spoke in sickly sweet voices, falsely cheerful, pretending to be friendly when really they were spying on me.

I'd brought a bunch of flowers with me, picking them up from the convenience store opposite the care home. I hadn't much time so I'd grabbed the first bunch I'd seen. I looked down at the straggly bunch of pink carnations in my hand. They wouldn't have been my first choice if I'd had more time, but I'm sure my mother would appreciate the sentiment anyway.

As I walked inside the care home, I was immediately surrounded by the stuffy warm air, laced with the smell of boiled vegetables. They had the radio on at the reception. Some kind of cheery Christmas song was blasting out of the speakers, the kind of song they play year after year until everyone is driven mad by it.

Sheila, the nurse I recognised from last time, got up from her chair behind the reception desk as I walked in. She pushed the visitors' book towards me. That's another irritation: the ridiculous fact that I have to sign a book when I want to see my own mother. But I bit my tongue, picked up the blue biro and scribbled my name in the box that Sheila pointed to.

"Have you seen this?" Sheila asked and pushed a small leaflet towards me, which had a cheap clip art image of a Christmas tree printed on it. "We're putting on Christmas lunch," she said. "We have space for a small number of relatives. I thought you might like to spend Christmas here with your mother. We do ask a small amount to cover the costs for non-residents." She pointed at the figure printed on the leaflet below the Christmas tree. Twenty pounds. What a rip-off!

I held my breath, so I didn't say something I would regret later.

"I'll have to think about it," I snapped after a pause, and the smile dropped from Sheila's face.

I intended to have my mother home by Christmas. There was no way we were going to spend Christmas here in this awful place.

"Let me show you to her room," Sheila said, walking around the counter towards me.

"I know the way. I have been here before."

"Yes, but we have had to move your mother since you last visited."

"You moved her?" The place was an absolute joke. She'd

only just gotten settled. Didn't they know how traumatic it was to get used to your surroundings and then have every-thing moved around again? I shook my head.

"Yes, she's got a nice room now. It's larger and looks out onto the back gardens rather than the main road."

"For goodness sake," I muttered.

Sheila was either oblivious to the furious expression on my face or deliberately ignored it. She opened a fire door onto a stairwell.

"You've put her upstairs?" My mother was perfectly capable of getting around herself, but stairs did give her trouble, and I hated the idea of her being stuck upstairs all the time. "What if she wanted to go out into the garden? She liked to walk around the grounds."

Sheila looked at me and wrinkled her nose. "It's Decem-ber, dear," she said as if that should quench all my protests.

Unbelievable. Did that mean as soon as summer was over they bundled all the residents indoors and refused to let them out again until spring?

My mother had always liked the outdoors and scarcely a day went by when she didn't go for a walk or potter in the garden.

The wave of guilt that rushed over me was over-whelming.

I gritted my teeth and followed Sheila upstairs.

Upstairs was even hotter. The radiators were blasting out heat. I shrugged off my coat, unable to bear it any more.

"This is her room," Sheila said in a sing-song voice.

Tucking my coat over my arm, I reached for the handle of the door to let myself in, but Sheila was quicker and pushed open the door and walked in before me.

"You've got a visitor, sweetheart," Sheila said in a patronising voice more suitable for addressing a child than a seventy-five-year-old woman.

My mother was sitting in a chair by the window. She had always been slim, but now her frame seemed impossibly frail. She hunched over in the blue velvet wing chair.

Her eyes swung towards me, and I felt a flutter of hope in my chest as I saw a dawning recognition in her eyes. Her mouth spread into a wide smile. "Hello, darling," she said.

My annoyance with Sheila was forgotten as I quickly crossed the room to my mother's side and gently kissed her cheek. "Hello, Mum. How have you been?"

"She recognises you. That's nice, isn't it?" Sheila interrupted.

I didn't bother to answer. I glanced down at my mother's hands, which were still bandaged, although not as heavily as before.

"How are your hands, mum? Are they getting better?"

My mother stared down at her hands and then blinked as if she was surprised to see that they were wrapped in bandages. She raised her hand and studied it carefully. She shrugged.

"Mustn't grumble," she said. "I'm sure they'll be right as rain in no time."

She smiled up at me. "Anyway, sit down and tell me what you've been up to."

I smiled back and perched on the edge of her bed.

"I've not seen you in ages, Alex. What kept you away?"

My breath froze in my lungs, and in the silence that followed I could hear the ticking of the clock on the wall. Tears started to sting my eyes.

Sheila's voice piped up, breaking the awkward silence. "Try not to let it bother you. They tend to confuse siblings. She'll probably recognise you later. It's very common."

My whole body was tense, and I longed to turn around and tell Sheila just what I thought of her inane twittering.

"We will be fine now," I said in a cold voice. "I'm sure you've got lots to do." I turned my back on her and didn't bother to turn around when she said goodbye and stepped outside.

I noticed that she didn't shut the door behind her.

"It's not Alex, Mum," I said. "It is me, Nicky."

Mum's eyes clouded with confusion, and I felt so cruel. I leaned forward, resting my elbows on my knees until my face was only a few inches away from my mother's.

"It's me, Nicky," I repeated, and I could hear the desperation in my own voice.

My mother's hand reached out to touch my cheek as she had done a thousand times before. Something in the movement triggered her memory.

"Of course, it is." She smiled. "Nicky."

"Yes, that's right."

I swallowed hard and wondered how much she remembered. Did she remember that Alex would never visit her?

Did she know, deep down, that she would never see Alex again?

CHAPTER THIRTY-THREE

CHARLOTTE CHECKED HER WATCH FOR what felt like the hundredth time. "Come on," she muttered under her breath.

She was waiting on the corner of Burnsey Road, some two streets away from where Lloyd Hughes lived with his mother. The response unit had gone straight there, but the rest of them had kept their distance, not wanting to alert anyone to the fact that the house was about to be raided.

Charlotte exchanged a glance with one of the uniformed officers who was going to be part of the team to search the property. They were all on edge, waiting for their cue.

When the radio crackled into life, Charlotte's pulse spiked. This was it: the breakthrough they'd been waiting for.

"We have access to the property," a crackly voice came over the radio.

"Do they have Lloyd Hughes in custody?" Charlotte asked the officer in charge of communications.

"Negative. Whereabouts of the suspect is unknown."

Charlotte clenched her fists. That wasn't the outcome they had hoped for. Had Lloyd Hughes known they were coming?

Once the communications officer had gotten clearance, the rest of the team headed over to the terraced house owned by Lloyd Hughes' mother.

It was a normal London street, lined with terraced houses. Cars were crammed into parking spaces. A few curtains twitched as they walked past. There was nothing to give any indication that a killer lived here. You could never tell what lurked beneath the surface and that was one of the first things Charlotte had learned in this job.

She was still buzzing with nervous energy.

One of the first response officers left the terraced house, walking down the small pathway to greet them on the pavement.

"It's cleared," he said. "You can start your search."

"Is there no sign of Lloyd Hughes at all?" Charlotte asked.

"There's only one little old lady in residence, and I severely doubt she is your killer." The officer smirked.

Charlotte muttered another curse.

"She is sitting on the sofa in the living room if you want a word," he said and headed back to the police van double-parked on the narrow street. His part of the task was complete, and he wasn't planning to hang around any longer than he had to.

As the other officers filed inside the terraced house to begin their search of the property, Charlotte went looking for Lloyd Hughes' mother.

She found her sitting on the sofa just as the first response officer had described. She was a small woman with light sandy hair that was greying at the temples. She wore a large burgundy cardigan, several sizes too big for her, and she was holding a tabby cat in her lap.

She turned to the doorway as Charlotte entered the living room.

"Mrs. Hughes?" Charlotte walked towards her. "My name is DC Charlotte Brown of the City of London police. I'm sure this must have all been a bit of a shock for you this morning, but I wonder if I could ask you a few questions."

Mrs. Hughes looked at her blankly for a moment and then nodded. "Are you going to tell me what's happening?" she asked in a whisper.

Charlotte nodded. "We are looking for Lloyd Hughes. Does he live at this address?"

"No, he hasn't done for a while."

"What is your relationship with Lloyd? Is he your son?"

Mrs. Hughes nodded. "Yes, that's right. Has he done something wrong?"

"We think Lloyd might be able to help us with an enquiry," Charlotte said carefully, not wanting to put Mrs. Hughes' back up and give her a reason to be defensive.

"Do you know where we might be able to find Lloyd, Mrs. Hughes?" Charlotte asked. "It is a matter of some urgency."

"Well, you'll have a job tracking him down. I last spoke to him two weeks ago."

"I see. Did he come to see you here?"

"No, he called me."

"And do you know where he was calling from?"

"Yes." Mrs. Hughes nodded.

This was like drawing blood out of a stone. Charlotte suppressed a sigh of frustration.

"Could you tell me where he was calling from?"

"I couldn't tell you exactly, but I know it was some-where in Thailand. He did tell me, but I can't remember the name of the place. It was something very foreign sounding."

Charlotte could practically see the case unravelling in front of her. "Thailand," she repeated. "And how long has he been there?"

"Two weeks," Mrs. Hughes said. "He's been travelling the world. He left England six months ago. He visited Australia first."

"Thank you, Mrs. Hughes. You've been very helpful."

Where on earth did they go from here? Mrs. Hughes might be lying, or her son could be lying to her about his whereabouts. That was something they could check out, but Charlotte had a horrible, sinking feeling that Lloyd Hughes really was in Thailand, which meant he wasn't their killer.

"I believe your son keeps snakes, is that correct?"

Mrs. Hughes pulled a face. "Yes, he did. He kept them in his bedroom. I didn't like it much, but you know boys, they need their hobbies."

Charlotte nodded. "We have traced an order for antivenom, which suggested Lloyd was keeping a partic-ular type of snake. Would you know the whereabouts of those snakes now?"

"There are no snakes here anymore, dear. He gave them all to a friend to look after before he left to go travelling."

Charlotte felt a flicker of hope. Perhaps all was not lost after all. If she could just get the name…

"Do you know the name of the person who took the snakes?"

Mrs. Hughes frowned and stroked the tabby cat in her lap. "Oh, I'm afraid I don't know who it was. They turned up in a van and took them away in a case. I was just relieved to see the snakes go to be honest."

"We need to search the property now," Charlotte said. "I'm very sorry for the inconvenience, but I promise we will keep the disruption to a minimum."

Mrs. Hughes looked put out. "Well, I can tell you that my Lloyd wouldn't have done anything wrong. He is a good boy."

Charlotte felt her mobile phone buzz in her pocket. She had put it on silent when they were waiting for the response team.

"I'll be back in just a moment," she said to Mrs. Hughes, standing up and striding out of the living room.

Outside on the street, Charlotte pulled her phone out of her pocket and answered it. It was Brookbank.

"What's happening?"

"It's not him, sir," Charlotte said. "Lloyd Hughes has been in Thailand for the past two weeks, and he's been out of the country for the past six months. That's according to his mother. Of course, we will need to double check, and make sure she's telling us the truth, but I believe her."

From the heavy silence on the other end of the line, Charlotte could sense Brookbank's disappointment.

She shivered and struggled to do up her coat one-handed. She decided to give him the rest of the bad news. "It gets worse. He's given the snakes to a friend, and we have no idea where they are."

CHAPTER THIRTY-FOUR

AFTER CHARLOTTE HAD FINISHED GIVING the bad news to Brookbank, she continued questioning Mrs. Hughes.

"I need you to tell me anything you can remember about Lloyd's friend. It's very important we find out where these venomous snakes are."

"Oh, no, dear. They weren't venomous." She shook her head so vigorously that the jowls on her neck wobbled. "I would never have allowed Lloyd to have venomous snakes in the house."

Charlotte frowned. This was going to be even harder then she'd anticipated. Mrs. Hughes had become agitated, and the tabby cat, sensing her unease, leapt out of her lap.

"Why don't I make a nice cup of tea?" Charlotte patted the woman's hand and smiled.

The search was continuing upstairs. Charlotte could hear them moving about as she slipped into the kitchen to make the tea. She could still see into the sitting room and saw that Mrs. Hughes hadn't moved from her spot on the sofa. She needed to keep an eye on her, but she didn't think it was likely that Mrs. Hughes would try to cover up or move any evidence. Charlotte was sure Mrs. Hughes genuinely believed the snakes had not been venomous.

While the kettle was boiling, Charlotte used her phone to get onto the Internet and take a screenshot of a photograph of a Russell's viper. She zoomed in to take a closer look and decided to save a couple more photographs. It was surprising how much individual vipers could vary in appearance.

She took two cups of tea back into the sitting room and handed one to Mrs. Hughes. Once she was sitting down, Charlotte said, "Did the snakes look anything like this?" She showed Mrs. Hughes the images on her phone.

Most of the vipers were sandy brown in colour with black markings.

Mrs. Hughes nodded her head. "Yes, he had one that looked like that." Mrs. Hughes pointed to one of the images.

"Okay," Charlotte said, deciding to get as much as she could from Mrs. Hughes without mentioning the fact that her son had kept one of the world's deadliest snakes in her house.

"Now, what can you tell me about the person who came to pick up the snakes? It's really important you remember everything you can for me."

"Well," Mrs. Hughes began, staring at the cat who was now sitting on an armchair grooming itself. "I remember they brought a big white van, and the snakes were in big glass tanks. They were locked up, but they still made my skin crawl. I made us both a cup of tea and we had chocolate digestives. We had a bit of a chat about the weather. It had been raining quite badly that morning and—"

"Do you remember anything about their appearance? Were they tall or short? Beard or clean-shaven?

Mrs. Hughes blinked at Charlotte. "Oh, dear. Did I give you the impression it was a man? How silly of me. It was a young woman who came to pick up the snakes."

CHAPTER THIRTY-FIVE

CHARLOTTE HADN'T CONSIDERED THE POSSIBILITY that the killer may have been female. Joe Griffin had been over six feet tall and very well built. Then there was the fact that the killer had somehow managed to overpower Tyler and kill Troy Scott. Was it really possible? Could the killer be female?

She rang the station and gave DCI Brookbank another update, letting him know they could now be looking for a woman.

It was possible that whoever had collected the snakes was an accomplice or a go-between. Perhaps she had sold the snakes, or even sold the venom. But Charlotte knew if they managed to track her down, they could be one step closer to stopping these horrific murders.

The next few hours passed slowly as the search team methodically made their way through every room in the house. Lloyd Hughes' mother sat in miserable silence until

Charlotte suggested she go next door to spend the afternoon with a neighbour.

Charlotte's thoughts drifted to DI Tyler. There had been no good news from the hospital, and Tyler's condition remained unchanged. The doctor had told them that head injuries varied considerably from case to case, and recovery was very difficult to predict. She decided to pop in on her way home after work. Tyler might not realise she was there, but she felt she owed him that. She knew DCI Brookbank had already visited.

"Find anything?" she asked PC Winters as he emerged from the cupboard under the stairs.

He shook his head. "No sign of any snakes or the venom. We've been through the loft now and unless he's managed to hide it in the cavity walls, there is no sign of the stuff. We have had the floorboards up in his old bedroom. Nothing looked like it had been disturbed, but we did the full search anyway. There's no sign of the antivenom anywhere either."

"Which means the woman must have taken it with her when she collected the snakes." Charlotte sighed.

Great. If she had taken Lloyd Hughes's supply of antivenom that would be one less way they were able to track her.

PC Winters gave an apologetic shrug.

"How much longer?" Charlotte asked.

"Another hour, maybe. Unless you think we need to dig up the garden?"

"I don't think that will be necessary."

She knew that most of the team now just wanted to call it a day. No one really believed they would find anything now. Their promising lead had come to a dead end.

* * *

By the time Charlotte was ready to go home for the evening, it was late and she feared she had missed the visiting hours at the Royal London Hospital in Whitechapel where Tyler was being treated.

Tyler had been moved from the trauma unit into ITU. When Charlotte arrived, she was dismayed to see there was nobody at his bedside or even waiting outside in the corridor. She knew he had split from his wife a few months ago, but when something like this happened people usually put aside their differences. It seemed terribly sad to see Tyler alone like this.

She sat down on the small chair beside Tyler's bed. He seemed smaller somehow, his hair even greyer. She knew that he had lost a lot of blood from his head wound, so she had expected him to look pale, but his skin was waxy and chalk white.

"The investigation isn't going well without you," Charlotte said. "I wish you could tell us what you were doing at Troy Scott's flat. Did you find out something? Did you see whoever it was before they hit you?"

She felt daft talking to him like that, but she'd heard somewhere that people in comas sometimes responded to the voices of people they knew.

"Brookbank has taken on the day-to-day running of the investigation now. He's still very keen on the school angle and the link between the victims. I looked at your notebook, by the way. Thanks for the detailed notes on the interview with Troy Scott. That was really helpful," she said sarcastically and glanced at the monitor that was measuring his vital signs.

Charlotte sighed heavily and leaned back in her chair. "We thought we had a lead today, but it turned out to be nothing."

The dim lights in the room were making Charlotte feel sleepy. After another few moments, she yawned and stood up. Reaching out, she patted DI Tyler's hand.

"I'm off now," she said. "I'll be back soon, and next time I expect to see you with your eyes open, okay?"

His hand felt cool and dry, and Charlotte squeezed his fingers, carefully avoiding the IV line in the back of his hand. "See you soon."

As Charlotte left the hospital, she got the same creepy feeling that she was being watched again and quickly turned to look over her shoulder. But at the hospital entrance beside the sliding doors, there was only an old man in pyjama bottoms and a dressing gown, smoking a cigarette and talking to a younger woman cradling a baby.

A paramedic headed through the sliding doors. There was nothing there out of the ordinary.

Charlotte tried to shake off her uneasy feeling and walked across the road, heading towards the underground station. She hadn't visited her nan in ages. It would be easy to cry off tonight, but she had promised to pop in after work, and she hated letting her down, so she got on the underground at Whitechapel station and headed for Mile End.

When she left the underground and walked out onto Mile End Road, it started to rain.

"Fantastic," she grumbled under her breath as she zipped up her coat and raised her hood. She should have brought her umbrella, but she couldn't stand carrying it around with her all the time.

She glanced back at the station just before she turned left into Burdett Road. There were lots of people around, but she didn't see anything untoward.

There was hardly anyone at the bus stop, which meant she had probably just missed the bus, but it wasn't a long walk to Selsey Street, so she lowered her head against the rain, stuffed her hands in her pockets and walked quickly.

By the time she got to Underhill house in Selsey Street, it was quiet. No one wanted to be out in this weather. She had checked frequently over her shoulder during the walk, but she couldn't shake the feeling she was being followed.

She'd been pretty good lately, getting that excessive checking of all her locks at home under control. She'd managed to cut down to one circuit of the flat, checking everything was secure, when she got in at night and one circuit when she left in the morning. She'd managed to whittle it down to just ten minutes now, whereas a few months ago she'd spent hours doing it.

She opened the door to the flats and entered the lobby. Ignoring the lift, she headed for the stairwell.

Charlotte hadn't been to the gym in over a week, so the least she could do was a little bit of stair climbing.

By the time she got to Nan's flat, she was panting for breath, reminding her just how unfit she really was.

She rang the bell and Nan answered quickly as if she had been hovering by the door.

"Hello, darling. Lovely to see you," Nan said as Charlotte leaned forward to kiss her cheek.

"Have you eaten yet? I've got a treat for you," Nan said without even waiting for an answer.

Charlotte closed the door behind her and followed Nan into the kitchen. She looked at the plastic bag on the kitchen counter with a parcel of food wrapped up in white paper and a tell-tale polystyrene cup.

"Aw, Nan, you shouldn't have," Charlotte said. "Maureen's?"

"Of course," Nan said. "I wouldn't get it from anywhere else."

Maureen's was a pie and mash shop in Chrisp Street. It had been there ever since Charlotte could remember, and Nan had always taken her there on Saturday when she'd been a young girl as Charlotte's mother used to work at the weekend.

Nan started to plate up the pie and mash, and lifted the small saucepan from the hob, which contained the liquor. Pie and mash just wasn't the same without it.

They had their pie and mash on trays in front of the TV, watching one of Nan's soaps.

Charlotte happily smothered her pie, mash and liquor with vinegar, her mouth watering in anticipation.

"Have you heard from your mum and dad?" Nan asked.

Charlotte nodded and tried to swallow a mouthful of piping hot mashed potato. "Last week," she said. "They are all right. They are having better weather over there at any rate."

"Are they coming back for Christmas?"

Charlotte shook her head. "They're going to stay in Spain. The flights over Christmas are ever so expensive."

After she had polished off the pie and mash, Charlotte took the plates to the kitchen and washed up. She was glad she had come to Nan's instead of going home to her empty flat. She didn't live far away, but she decided she would stay here tonight. It would be nice to spend the evening relaxing and watching the telly with Nan before falling asleep.

And a relaxing evening was exactly what she needed tonight. She needed to unwind and de-stress, as she knew she had one hell of a day in front of her tomorrow.

CHAPTER THIRTY-SIX

MACKINNON DIDN'T GET HOME TO Oxford until after midnight. When he let himself in, he found Chloe dozing on the sofa. A half-full wine glass was in front of her on the coffee table.

She stirred as he walked into the room and smiled sleepily at him. "Hi."

"Any left?" Mackinnon asked, nodding at her wine glass as he sat down beside her on the sofa.

Chloe stretched and moved her feet to rest them on Mackinnon's legs.

"Sorry, there's only a dribble left. I needed it tonight, but I can open another one if you want."

Mackinnon shook his head. He knew he needed to get some sleep otherwise he was going to regret it in the morning. "How is Katy?"

Chloe groaned. "I don't understand that girl. I've been

trying to get it out of her all evening, but she won't tell me anything. I still have no idea what went on, although I know she's the one in trouble with the headmistress."

Mackinnon frowned. It didn't make sense. This whole thing didn't fit Katy's personality. She was always so well behaved, achieving top grades and she was in the top sets for all of her subjects at school. Was Katy just acting out because no one was listening to her or dealing with the situation?

Mackinnon changed his mind about the wine and went to open another bottle of red Shiraz. Chloe followed him into the kitchen.

"So what did the headmistress say on the phone? What does she want to talk about tomorrow?" Mackinnon asked as he poured the wine.

Chloe exhaled a long sigh. "Katy's punishment."

Mackinnon shook his head and took a sip of his wine. He couldn't be bothered to wait for it to breathe. Punishment? What on earth had Katy done?

Mackinnon knew he had a long day ahead of him tomorrow and should have headed to bed, but despite that, he and Chloe stayed up talking until the early hours of the morning.

When Chloe could barely keep her eyes open and they had finished the bottle of wine Mackinnon had opened, he got to his feet and pulled Chloe up from the sofa. "Come on," he said. "We have to get to bed or we will never get up in the morning. It's not going to look good if we're late for our visit to the headmistress."

Chloe looped her arms around his waist. "You do know

that I appreciate you coming back, don't you? I know you are in the middle of a big case at work."

"Work can wait," Mackinnon said and gently kissed her forehead. "This is more important."

CHAPTER THIRTY-SEVEN

CHARLOTTE WOKE UP LATE THE next morning. She'd slept like a log at Nan's and then had to scurry around quickly, showering and throwing on her clothes in record time. She thanked her lucky stars that she had kept some of her clothes at Nan's for when she stayed over, so she didn't have to go back home to get changed.

Nan was still in her nightdress, sipping a cup of tea when Charlotte left.

She raced out of the flat and down the stairs. As she exited onto Selsey Street, she was moving so fast that she almost ran into a woman with long, dark hair. A woman who looked strangely familiar.

Charlotte stopped abruptly and stared at her. "Have you been following me?" she demanded.

Charlotte felt a rush of satisfaction as she realised that she hadn't been imagining things.

The woman lifted a hand and tucked a lock of hair

behind her ear, keeping her eyes fixed on the floor. "Yeah, sorry about that, but I need your advice."

Charlotte gritted her teeth. She didn't have time for this. She folded her arms across her chest and said, "I'm in a rush. I'm late for work."

"But you know him," the woman said. "And I need your help. I keep doing things that annoy him." She looked up at Charlotte with tear-filled eyes. "I don't mean to, but I seem to have rubbed him up the wrong way…"

Charlotte felt herself softening towards the woman. This was the same woman her ex-boyfriend had brought to Charlotte's flat a few months ago, flaunting his new relationship. She was sure he intended to make her feel jealous but Charlotte hadn't felt the slightest spark of jealousy, instead, she felt terribly sorry for her. It had been obvious it was going to end up like this. Charlotte's ex was a cruel and abusive bully.

Charlotte took a deep breath and then said, "I can give you the number of a counsellor at a women's crisis centre. She can help you. If you want to leave him—"

"What?" The woman's voice was sharp, and she stared at Charlotte angrily. For the first time, she raised her face and Charlotte inhaled sharply as she saw the bruise beneath the woman's cheekbone.

"I don't want to leave him," she said. "I just want your advice on how I can stop making him angry. You were with him for a long time. I just want to know how to make him happy."

Charlotte took a step back and shook her head. What the hell?

"I'll give you some advice," she said. "But it's not the

advice you're looking for. You need to wake up. He is nothing but a bully, and you will never make him happy. You're wasting your time and you should get out while you can. I'm guessing that bruise was from him."

Charlotte raised a hand, but the woman slapped it away.

"I should've guessed you would say that," the woman spat. "You want him back yourself, don't you?"

Charlotte stared at her for a moment, unable to reply. *Unbelievable.*

"Don't be so bloody ridiculous." Charlotte started to walk away. "And stay away from me in future."

Furious, Charlotte stalked off in the direction of St Paul's Way and didn't look back.

CHAPTER THIRTY-EIGHT

AT EIGHT THIRTY SHARP, CHLOE and Mackinnon sat in Mrs. Doyle's office. Mrs. Doyle was the sharp-faced head-mistress of Katy's school.

"Now, I've asked you here today to discuss Katy," Mrs. Doyle began in a soft Scottish accent. "Because of the serious nature of Katy's actions, I believe I would be well within my rights to exclude her. But I'm willing to take her recent troubles into consideration. I think some time away from school and a stern talking to from her parents would make her realise the gravity of her actions."

"I'm sorry," Chloe interrupted. "Would you mind telling us exactly what Katy is supposed to have done?"

Mrs. Doyle pursed her lips, then said, "It's a rather serious situation. Katy's class has been studying business models for economics. One of their tasks has been to prepare items to sell at break times. The idea is to generate a profit and understand things like turnover and profit margins. Most of the children, Katy included, have opted to sell things like cakes."

Mackinnon guessed that Chloe must have known about this, but it was news to him.

"Katy made fairy cakes," Mrs. Doyle said. "We had a situation yesterday when a girl from Katy's class was taken seriously ill. She had a rather nasty stomach upset. We found out that Katy had added laxatives to the cakes."

Chloe blinked and then looked at Mackinnon. He was lost for words.

"As I'm sure you can understand, we have to take this very seriously. The girl's mother is understandably extremely upset," Mrs. Doyle said.

"Are you absolutely sure that Katy did this?" Mackinnon asked.

Mrs. Doyle nodded. "Katy admitted as much yesterday. Perhaps it would be a good idea to get her in here to explain."

Chloe nodded numbly and Mrs. Doyle got to her feet, walked around her large desk and opened the door. Katy, whom they had left sitting outside beside the secretary's desk, came in with a sullen look on her face, refusing to look at Mackinnon or her mother.

"Did you do what Mrs. Doyle said?" Chloe's voice was shaky and Mackinnon wasn't sure whether she was close to tears or just absolutely furious.

When Katy didn't reply, Chloe tried again. "Did you put laxatives into the cake?"

Katy looked up, defiant. "Yes! She deserved it, and I'm glad I did it."

Chloe looked taken aback and even Mrs. Doyle looked shocked.

"You told me I shouldn't run away from my problems, so I was just sticking up for myself. You wouldn't help me, the teachers don't help either," Katy said, pausing to shoot an accusing look at Mrs. Doyle.

"Don't be so stupid. I can't believe you would have done something like this," Chloe said.

Katy promptly burst into tears. She got up so suddenly that she knocked the chair to the floor as she fled the room.

Mackinnon's phone was on silent, but he could feel it buzzing in his pocket. "I won't be a moment," he said and left Chloe and Mrs. Doyle talking in the office.

Mackinnon headed straight for the exit, and just outside he found Katy leaning against the wall.

At first, he thought she was going to yell at him again, but she didn't. She quickly stepped forward and leaned her forehead against his chest.

She started to sob. "Please don't make me come back here, Jack. *Please.*"

CHAPTER THIRTY-NINE

AN HOUR AND A HALF later, Mackinnon arrived at Wood Street station. He threw his jacket over the back of his chair and sat down, powering up his computer, ready to start work.

But he didn't get very far.

DCI Brookbank poked his head out of his office and waved Mackinnon over. "We have got the warrant for that weekend paper, the one we think was printing the obituaries. The owner is a woman called Lorraine Collier. She may give us a bit of grief. She is very anti-police from what I have learned from DC Webb."

Brookbank's mouth spread into a wide grin. "That's why I have decided to send you. You'll have to lay on the charm, Jack."

Mackinnon took the paperwork from Brookbank's outstretched hand. "Great," he said without enthusiasm. "I'll go there now, shall I?"

He opened the file and looked at the address on the front page.

"No time like the present," Brookbank said. "Did everything go all right this morning?"

Mackinnon hadn't gone into detail about why he needed to start late today. Before meeting with the headmistress that morning, he'd had no idea what Katy had been up to anyway, and he didn't want to start explaining things to Brookbank now. They had too much work to do.

"It went fine," Mackinnon said.

Brookbank nodded, satisfied, and Mackinnon headed out to track down Lorraine Collier.

* * *

The outside of the building that housed the weekend paper wasn't exactly impressive, and the inside was even less so.

Lorraine Collier was running the paper out of a solitary office over a fish and chip shop in Whitechapel. It was just off the Whitechapel Road and took Mackinnon only minutes to walk there from the tube station. As he passed the Royal London Hospital, he thought of Tyler. He'd heard that morning that Tyler remained unconscious and it was still touch-and-go.

Lorraine Collier took her sweet time answering the intercom. After Mackinnon gave his name, he had to repeat it numerous times before she buzzed him in.

Rather than greet him by the door, she stood at the top of the stairs, blocking the doorway to the office as if she was standing guard.

She was a tall woman with curly hair bordering on

frizzy. Her eyes were close-set and she gave Mackinnon a severe look as he approached the door.

"No warrant means no names," she snapped.

Mackinnon smiled and held up the paperwork. "That's not going to be a problem. Let's go inside and have a chat."

He gestured to the small office behind Lorraine Collier. There were two desks crammed into the small room, one of them was occupied by a young girl of around twenty. As the girl had the same frizzy hair as Lorraine Collier and the same pointed nose, Mackinnon guessed it must be her daughter.

"Go and get yourself a coffee, Lillian," Mrs. Collier said.

After eyeballing Mackinnon in obvious curiosity, Lillian grabbed her handbag and left the office.

"Was that your daughter?" Mackinnon asked.

Lorraine Collier pursed her lips and then made a tutting sound. "Let's not waste time," she said. "I'd like to see the warrant, please."

Mackinnon handed her the papers. "Of course."

After she had spent some minutes reading the documents, Mackinnon said, "I think you will find everything is in order."

She looked up sharply and then scowled. "Fine." She flung the paperwork down on the desk. "Knock yourself out. It's all yours." She gestured to the computer on her desk and the untidy piles of paper and gave Mackinnon a smug smile.

"I would appreciate it if you could give me the name of the person who ordered the obituaries for Beverley Madison, Joe Griffin and Troy Scott."

"It's all there," she said. "Somewhere. I'm sure it won't

take a smart chap like you very long to find it. There's a filing cabinet too. You're welcome to go through that as well. I'll just sit over here." She went and sat at her daughter's desk, crossing her legs, smiling and looking very pleased with herself.

Mackinnon didn't have time for this. He didn't know what Lorraine Collier's personal issue with the police was, but she obviously had some kind of agenda.

"It would be a lot quicker, and I'd be out of your hair a lot sooner if you could find it for me," Mackinnon said.

"I don't doubt it." Lorraine Collier gave him a cold smile. "But I'm not going to do your job for you."

Mackinnon exhaled a long slow breath and did his best to smile at the woman. She was now really irritating him. "Do we have a problem here? You obviously have an issue with the police. Or is it just me?"

"Why would I have a problem with a corrupt dictatorial police system?" Her voice grew shrill. "Why would I object to things like racial profiling, to a police force that stops and searches based on the colour of someone's skin?" She was really warming to her theme now.

"I don't have time for this," Mackinnon said. "I'm sorry if this offends your principles, but right now, I'm trying to locate a killer before anyone else gets hurt. Three people have already been killed. Those three people all had obituaries posted in your paper before they died."

Lorraine Collier looked uncomfortable. Mackinnon knew that this wasn't news to her. DC Webb had already explained why they needed the names.

"I'm cooperating, aren't I?" Lorraine Collier said in a

belligerent tone. She folded her arms over her chest, but Mackinnon saw the brief hesitation on her face.

"Three people, Lorraine. Three people with families and friends left behind. Don't you care about their families? Don't you think they deserve justice?"

Lorraine Collier glanced at the window and then back at Mackinnon. She bit down on her lower lip and then said. "There were four."

"Four?"

Lorraine Collier nodded. Mackinnon held his breath and waited for her to continue.

Lorraine shrugged. "The same person ordered four names. All at the same time. I thought you knew that."

"What was the fourth name?"

She swallowed, but still made no move towards the computer.

"If you don't hand over that name right now, I'm going to hold you personally responsible if that fourth person is killed. Do you understand me?"

Lorraine Collier blinked rapidly and then she finally moved to the seat behind her computer and tapped on the keyboard. She opened up a file.

"All four names came in from the same order ID number, but I don't actually have the name of the buyer, the person who ordered the obituaries. The paper has been struggling recently, and sales have been down. I was looking at ways to increase our revenue. One of the marketing ideas I had was to offer people free adverts or family notices in the hope that they would go on and pay for further adverts the following month." She screwed up her face. "So far it hasn't worked very well."

"Why can't you give me the name of the person who ordered these obituaries?"

"Because nobody actually paid, so we don't have a financial record. I have an email address. I can give you that."

Mackinnon nodded. It wasn't what they needed, but it was better than nothing.

The woman pressed a few buttons on the keyboard and the printer hummed into life beside Mackinnon.

"Now," Mackinnon said. "I need the fourth name please. The name the other obituary was ordered for."

"Lauren Hicks. The last obituary was ordered for Lauren Hicks."

Mackinnon leaned forward so that he could see the name on the computer screen for himself. "This is the obituary they wanted to post?" he asked, pointing at the screen.

Lorraine Collier nodded. "Yes, they were very specific in their wording. It's exactly what they asked for."

"I need anything you can tell me that might help us identify her, find out where she lives," Mackinnon said. "We need to track her down."

They needed to find her fast. It could already be too late.

"I haven't got an address," she said. "But I think she must have worked in some kind of legal profession. It says here in the obituary that she will be sadly missed by her colleagues and never forgotten for her work in the legal field."

Mackinnon leaned forward again and scanned the contents of the obituary. "Can you print me a copy, please?"

Lorraine Collier did as he asked as Mackinnon loomed over her.

She handed Mackinnon the sheets of printer paper and he looked down again at the name. Lauren Hicks. He needed to call this in now and hope they weren't already too late.

Mackinnon called DC Collins straight away. "I've got a new name," Mackinnon said without preamble. "There was another obituary ordered by the same person."

"I wasn't expecting that," Collins said, and Mackinnon could hear him fumbling around on his desk for a pen. "Name?"

"Lauren Hicks. I think she has some kind of job in the legal field. The obituary mentions her contributions."

"Right," Collins said. "I'll check it out now."

There was a pause and Mackinnon could hear Collins tapping on the keyboard. After a moment, Collins said, "I think I've got a match. Lauren Hicks is on the school records, the same year as the others. Born June 1976. Luckily for us she didn't get married and change her name."

"Address?"

"I'm looking now... Got it!"

"Great," Mackinnon said. "Let Brookbank know, and get a team there straight away. She is definitely the next target."

CHAPTER FORTY

I WATCHED LAUREN HICKS CLIMB out of the taxi as I stood at the bus stop across the street. Even from this distance, I recognised her easily. She had tucked her hair behind her ears, the same thing she used to do when she was fifteen. It made her ears stick out and made her a target for teasing at school.

Out of all of them, Lauren seemed the most familiar. She hadn't changed much in the intervening years. Even her hairstyle was the same.

Beverley Madison had highlighted her hair and had it cut into a short, layered style. She'd also had some cosmetic work done, which had given her bloated lips and the kind of plump cheeks that didn't look natural. When I'd confronted her at the hotel, it was hard to see past all that to the schoolgirl she had been.

When Joe Griffin had been at school, his hair had been his crowning glory. He'd grown it long, taking pride in his floppy fringe. He'd worn it in a curtain style, parted down the middle. When I'd seen him in the car park, he was thinning on top, and it wouldn't have been long before he was completely bald.

Troy Scott had aged the worst. I would never have recognised him if I had passed him on the street. It was only down to diligent research that I was able to track him. His lifestyle probably hadn't helped. Sitting behind a computer screen all day hadn't been good to him.

But none of them had to worry about getting any older now.

I smiled, but the smile soon slid from my face when I saw Lauren Hicks had pulled a baby basket out of the back of the taxi. I felt my body stiffen.

I hadn't known about the baby.

It made me uncomfortable. But Lauren hadn't shown any sympathy back then, so why should I? Besides, the baby wouldn't remember a thing.

I shifted the bag between my hands. It was surprisingly heavy. I'd spent some time debating whether to bring it. It did seem a little dramatic, but as this was to be the last one, I wanted it to be the best.

I put my hand in my coat pocket and felt the smooth paper of the obituary.

I took a deep breath. Everything was ready. I was prepared.

It was time to go to work one last time.

CHAPTER FORTY-ONE

LAUREN HICKS JUGGLED HER LAPTOP bag, handbag and the baby bassinet as she let herself into her terraced townhouse.

She had only popped into Chambers today to say hello to her colleagues. The first step in getting back to work. She had been away for six months and getting back into the routine was going to take some adjustment. Her plan today had been to test the waters slowly. She had left baby Mia at the nursery for the first time, just for a couple of hours, then had a meeting with some of the senior members of the Chambers, followed by the annual Christmas lunch with the firm.

She'd left them there still drinking. The day had dragged, and she had been so glad to see Mia safe and sound and gurgling happily at the nursery.

She had managed to convince herself that Mia would

have been crying all day, but the nursery staff said she had been a perfect angel.

Lauren looked around at the state of her kitchen. Returning to work was going to be harder than she'd thought. She had been in such a rush to get ready that morning, she hadn't done any washing-up or even tidied away the breakfast things.

Mia started to squirm, so she put her in her favourite little bouncy chair, keeping her in the kitchen so she could keep an eye on her as she tidied up.

Mia had seemed perfectly happy at the nursery, and of course Lauren was glad she hadn't been distressed, but at the same time, she would have liked to have been missed just a little bit.

She bundled a load of washing into the machine and sighed. How on earth was she going to get through all this and work at the same time? There just weren't enough hours in the day.

She had just switched the machine on and straightened up when there was a knock at the door.

"Who could that be?" Lauren said to Mia. "We're not expecting anyone, are we?"

Mia kicked her legs and bounced happily in the chair.

Lauren could see a dark shape in front of the misted glass panel in the front door. She shivered and had a strange feeling that she should ignore whoever it was and pretend she wasn't in.

She tucked her hair behind her ears and gave herself a little mental shake. She was being quite ridiculous.

When she opened the door, her first reaction was panic.

She put her hand to her chest. "What is it? What's wrong?"

On the doorstep, stood two uniformed police officers.

"Nothing to worry about," the female officer said. "My name is Jane, PC Jane Worthington and this is my colleague PC Brian Bright. We're just here to check on you. Is everything okay?"

Lauren nodded, and her panic started to recede as the officers showed their ID. There had obviously been some kind of mix-up. The officers had come to the wrong house.

"Everything is fine here," she said. "I think you might have the wrong address."

"Are you Lauren Hicks?"

Lauren swallowed nervously and nodded.

"Is it okay if we come in and have a chat inside?"

Lauren stood back and let the officers enter. She collected Mia from the kitchen, scooping her from the bouncy chair and carried her into the front room. The officers sat down on the sofa, and Lauren sat on an armchair, balancing Mia on her knee.

"What's going on?" Lauren asked.

"Your name has come up as part of an ongoing investigation."

"I can assure you I've never done anything illegal. I think there must have been some kind of mix-up."

"We are here purely as a precaution. I don't want you to worry. You could be a target of someone we have been investigating."

"What? Who?"

"I'm afraid I don't have all the details, madam, but a detective will be here shortly to explain the situation. Just to be on the safe side, we're going to stay here with you. PC Bright will be stationed outside in the police car, and I'll stay with you in the house."

Lauren nodded numbly. She had absolutely no idea what this could be about. Despite working as administration support for a legal team, when it came down to it she was just as scared as anyone else would be.

PC Bright stood up. "I'll be outside in the car."

PC Jane Worthington nodded, and when he had left the room, she said, "Have you received any unusual notes recently?"

Lauren shook her head. Who would want to target her? This didn't make any sense. "What is the investigation about?"

"Have you been following the news?"

"Not really." Lauren hadn't had a chance to watch the news in ages. She hadn't even had five minutes to spare to put up the Christmas decorations. It would be Mia's first Christmas, and she'd wanted to make it special, to prove that despite the fact she was a single mum, she could make Christmas perfect for the two of them.

She didn't want Mia to watch TV all day like some kids, so Lauren never put it on during the day.

Although, she looked forward to her time in front of the TV once she had put Mia to bed, she could never stay awake long enough to watch anything. Five minutes after switching it on she was dozing on the sofa.

As PC Worthington cooed over Mia, Lauren wondered if she would ever stop feeling tired. Perhaps when Mia turned eighteen?

They were disturbed by a crackle on the radio. Lauren

could have sworn she heard a voice say, "Up the garden path," and she wondered if that was some kind of police code.

"That was PC Bright," the female police officer said. She looked over her shoulder towards the window. "There's nothing to worry about—"

A knock at the front door made Lauren jump.

Before Lauren could stand up, PC Worthington put her hand on Lauren's shoulder. "I'll get it," she said and walked out of the sitting room into the hallway.

Lauren followed the police officer, carrying Mia on her hip, but remained a safe distance from the front door.

PC Worthington opened the front door and said, "Can I help you?"

Lauren inched forward so she could see the visitor.

When she got a glimpse, Lauren smiled. "Oh, it's okay, officer. It's perfectly safe."

PC Worthington took a step back and looked at Lauren. "You know each other?"

Lauren nodded. "Old friends."

PC Worthington moved to the side so that she was no longer blocking the doorway. "Fine. It will be nice for you to have a familiar face around." She closed the door behind the visitor.

Lauren headed into the living room. "Come in. I haven't seen you in ages. How have you been?"

"I'll make some tea and let you two catch up," PC Worthington said. "That's if you don't mind me using your kitchen."

Lauren shrugged. To be honest, she wasn't interested in

tea. She just wanted some answers, but it didn't seem like she was going to get any until the detective arrived.

After PC Worthington left them alone in the living room, Lauren turned to her visitor. "Nicky, this was certainly a surprise. You won't believe the day I have had."

CHAPTER FORTY-TWO

LAUREN HICKS ACTUALLY LOOKED LIKE she was happy to see me.

That wouldn't last long.

I walked across to her, put down my bag and held my arms out for the baby. "What a cutie."

Lauren handed the baby to me with a smile.

I sat down in an armchair and looked down into the baby's pink face. "What's her name?"

Lauren stood over me, looking every inch the proud mother. "Mia."

The black holdall I had put on the floor moved.

Lauren gasped. Her eyes widened and she shot me a worried glance, opening her mouth. I'm sure she was just about to ask me what was in the bag, but what she saw next froze the question on her lips.

I had pulled out the syringe from my pocket, and I held it menacingly close to the baby's chubby thigh.

"What...? What are you doing?" Her voice cracked as she took a step towards me, fear burning in her eyes.

My voice was emotionless. "Don't come any closer unless you want me to hurt the baby."

Confusion and hurt mixed on her face as her eyes desperately searched mine for some kind of clue, an explanation.

This really had been a surprise. She hadn't been expecting me. Had she not heard about the other victims?

"Have you been following the news?" I said casually, keeping the syringe close to the baby as she gurgled in my arms.

Lauren didn't answer, she seemed almost frozen with fear. Eventually, she stuttered, "Please... Please don't hurt her. I'll do anything."

"Keep your voice down," I said.

My own voice was barely above a whisper. I didn't know how long the police officer would leave us alone. Not that it really mattered. I didn't care if I was caught now. Lauren was the last one.

I didn't want to hurt the police officer, and I would never have harmed the baby. But I was open to using all the tools at my disposal, and baby Mia made an excellent bargaining chip.

"Have you heard about the Charmer?"

"The Charmer?" Lauren repeated blankly, and then something in her expression changed and her eyes widened. "It was you... The murder?"

"There was more than one murder." Lauren was irritating me now. The whole country was following the case, reading about it over their cornflakes every morning. The news story had been on every news channel. How could she have missed it?

"I like the snake part, don't you? Particularly apt, don't you think?"

Lauren's hand flew to her mouth, and she looked at the black holdall I had brought with me, which was now still.

"But why me, Nicky? Why would you target me? I don't understand."

I gritted my teeth. How could she think I wouldn't target her? Hers had been the greatest betrayal of them all. Now she needed to pay.

I looked down at the baby who was kicking her chubby legs. I felt a twinge of panic and moved the syringe out of reach.

I shook my head. "She trusted you. She thought you were her friend."

"I was!" Lauren said desperately, wringing her hands. "I didn't have anything to do with it. I—"

I cut her off. "You were there." I stared at her with hatred.

I'd admired her once. I thought she was amazing, everything I wanted to be. I'd loved the clothes she'd worn, the music she'd listened to. I'd looked up to her.

"Nicky, you've got it wrong. I tried to help her. I would never have hurt Alex."

This was hard. In comparison, Beverley Madison, Joe Griffin and Troy Scott's murders had been easy. I'd never known them, unlike Lauren. But I couldn't trust her. She would say anything she could to protect her baby.

I raised an eyebrow. "Really?"

Lauren nodded frantically, completely oblivious to the

sarcasm in my voice. "If you can just give me a chance to explain. I'll tell you everything. I'll tell you exactly what happened that day."

I relaxed my grip on the syringe slightly, moving it away from the baby's leg. "Go on then," I said. "Explain."

We didn't have much time. The policewoman would soon be back with the tea, but I needed to hear this.

Lauren looked up at the ceiling. Her chest was rising and falling fast. "It was horrible," she said. "But I really believe no one meant for her to die."

"But she did, didn't she?" I spat out, before taking a breath and trying to calm down. I needed to stay in control.

Lauren looked down at baby Mia in my lap and her lip wobbled. "It started in our science class. We were giving a presentation and we had to work in pairs. As usual, I was working with Alex. For some reason, Mrs. Diamond, the science teacher, insisted Alex would have to do her share of the talking. She knew about Alex's lisp, but she didn't care. She had given us the topic of snakes as well, which made it even harder for Alex."

"Get to the point." I had a feeling Lauren was stalling. Perhaps she thought that the policewoman would save her.

"You know her lisp got worse when she was stressed, but Mrs. Diamond said Alex had to face up to her problems otherwise she'd never get past them."

Lauren's gaze flickered back to the baby. "Please, let me take Mia. I'll still tell you the rest. I'll tell you everything. You don't have to hurt her."

She thought I was an idiot. As soon as I handed her the baby, Lauren would run out to the kitchen screaming for help.

I glanced at the clock on the mantelpiece. They had said the detective was on his way over, but I had no idea what time he would arrive.

"Just get on with it, Lauren," I said. "And I will decide if anyone gets hurt."

Lauren shivered. "Alex tried to give the talk, but of course she lisped and everyone in the class laughed. It was horrible. She ran out crying. I didn't know what to do. I wanted to go after her, but Mrs. Diamond forbade it."

Lauren drew a shaky breath and I leaned forward.

"After the lesson was over, I saw Alex in the corridor. She had left her bag in the classroom and needed to get it before the next lesson." Lauren's voice wobbled slightly, and I held my breath.

"Alex was packing away her things when a group of kids decided they hadn't teased her enough. It was Beverley, Troy and Joe. You must remember what they were like, they walked round the school as if they owned the place. They crowded around Alex and pushed her into the supply cupboard at the back of the classroom. I should have helped her, but I was scared. I didn't want to get locked in there too."

I forced myself to take a breath. I knew what was coming next.

"Then Troy thought it would be a good idea to torment her further. He threw something in the cupboard and then shut the door again. It was dark in there, and Alex wouldn't have been able to see, but he told her he'd put his snake in there with her. We all knew that Troy kept snakes. Alex started to scream. They locked the door and ran off with the key, laughing."

Lauren rubbed her hands over her pale face. "I tried to shout and tell Alex that it was okay. I told Alex it wasn't really a snake. I think Troy had thrown in a bit of old skipping rope. But she was screaming so much, she didn't hear me. I went to try and get help, and I ran straight into Mrs. Diamond. It was lunchtime, and she'd just made herself a coffee. I told her everything, that Alex was locked in the cupboard and that the other kids had taken the key. I begged her to come with me, but she said she needed to finish her coffee first…"

Lauren shook her head. "I didn't know what to do. I should have made more of a fuss, or gone to another teacher, but I didn't." Lauren stared at me, her eyes wide and pleading. "I couldn't make her come. I was just a kid, and she was a teacher."

"Here we go. Two cups of tea." The cheerful voice of the policewoman made me jump. I shifted my position so that she couldn't see the syringe and shot Lauren a warning glance.

"Thank you," I said as the policewoman set the mug of tea on the coffee table in front of me.

"Ah, look at that. She's fallen asleep."

I looked down at baby Mia and saw that the policewoman was right, she had fallen asleep. I hadn't noticed. I had been so intent on hearing the rest of Lauren's story.

"If you two are okay, I'll take a cup of tea down to PC Bright. He'll sulk if he doesn't get a cup."

"We're fine, aren't we, Lauren?"

Lauren nodded and plastered a fake smile on her face.

I waited until after I'd heard the policewoman shut the door and then turned back to Lauren. "Carry on."

"I went back to the classroom, but it was quiet. Alex wasn't screaming anymore. I sat down beside the cupboard and waited. Eventually Mrs. Diamond arrived and she unlocked the door. That was when we saw her... Alex was lying on the floor. She'd had an asthma attack."

I looked away so that Lauren couldn't see my reaction. I knew the part about the asthma attack, but at the inquest they'd ruled it was an accident. I knew it wasn't. It was brought on by what they did. How could that be classified as an accident?

When I turned back, I saw that Lauren had moved closer. She reached out a shaking hand to touch the baby's cheek.

Her eyes locked with mine. "I tried my best. I know I let her down. I'm so sorry."

I didn't reply, but I stood up and shoved the baby into her arms. I grabbed the large black holdall and its squirming contents and headed towards the front door.

There had been a change of plan.

CHAPTER FORTY-THREE

MACKINNON SPOTTED THE MARKED CAR parked outside Lauren Hicks' residence as he turned into St Andrews Close. He parked behind them and watched as a female police officer passed a steaming mug to the male officer sitting behind the wheel.

Hearing Mackinnon slam the car door, the female officer straightened up and turned around to face him.

"DS Mackinnon," he said, flashing his ID. "Everything okay in there?" He glanced towards the house.

"PC Jane Worthington," she said holding out her hand. "PC Bright is in the car. Everything is fine. Lauren Hicks has a friend with her."

Mackinnon headed towards the house and rang the front doorbell.

PC Worthington scrambled to catch up. "She's fine. I only left her for a minute to take PC Bright his tea." She glanced back at the marked car.

Mackinnon didn't answer. He knocked again, feeling uneasy.

PC Worthington chewed on her fingernails. "Maybe I should have left the door on the latch, but it's so cold today, and she has a little baby…"

He took a step back and tried to peer through the lace curtains surrounding the bay window. He could just make out a figure sitting on the sofa.

He rapped on the window, and slowly the figure turned and then stood up.

When Lauren Hicks opened the door, Mackinnon immediately knew something had happened. Her face was pinched and drawn, and she was clutching the baby as if she was afraid someone might take it from her.

She shrank back from the door as Mackinnon entered.

"It's all right, Lauren, this is the detective I told you about," PC Worthington said, craning her neck to try and look inside the sitting room. "Where is your friend?"

Lauren didn't respond.

"Lauren, I'm Detective Sergeant Jack Mackinnon. I'm here to try and explain the situation to you. Is it all right if we go into the sitting room and have a chat?"

"You're too late," she said, her voice monotone.

"What do you mean?" Mackinnon asked.

"She has already been," Lauren said. "You're looking for the Charmer, aren't you?"

Mackinnon tried to stay calm. "Shall we go inside?"

The front door was still open and the cold air was seeping inside the house. Lauren Hicks was only wearing a thin blouse.

Lauren nodded and turned around, walking back into the living room in a daze.

"Are you telling me that the lady that came to see you was the Charmer?" PC Worthington's face turned pale.

"I think we could do with another cup of tea," Mackinnon said, looking at the female officer meaningfully.

"We haven't finished the last one yet."

Mackinnon glared at her.

"Oh, right. I see. Cup of tea coming up," she said, finally getting the message.

Mackinnon sat on the edge of the sofa, leaning forward, resting his elbows on his knees and studying Lauren.

She was staring down at the baby and a big fat teardrop ran down her cheek.

"Tell me what happened, Lauren."

Lauren looked up and swallowed hard. "She came here. She had a syringe and she picked up Mia. I thought she was going to…" The rest of her words were smothered with a sob.

"Who was here, Lauren? Can you give me her name?"

"It was Nicky."

"Do you know her last name?"

"Nicola Brent. We were at school together. I was her sister's best friend. It was her. All of it. She killed them all."

"When did she leave?"

"Just now. Just after the police officer took a cup of tea to the man in the car."

When PC Worthington entered the room bringing Mackinnon his cup of tea, he took the opportunity to go out into the hall and phone Collins to fill him in.

He walked back into the living room just as PC Worthington was trying to convince Lauren to let her take the sleeping baby from her arms.

"She stays with me," Lauren snapped.

"That's fine," Mackinnon said. "I want you to tell me everything that happened. Did she hurt either of you?"

Lauren shook her head. "No, but she had a syringe and I thought she was going to inject Mia. I tried to tell her I had nothing to do with her sister's death. She didn't believe me at first."

"What did you tell Nicky?"

"The truth. Her sister got bullied at school because she had a lisp. A group of kids locked her in a cupboard, and she had an asthma attack. I was there, but I didn't get her help in time."

Lauren bit down on her lip and hugged the baby to her chest. "Beverley was the ringleader. She could be really nasty. Joe worshipped the ground she walked on and would have done anything she said, but it was Troy who pretended to throw the snake in the cupboard. I think that is what triggered the asthma attack."

"You told all this to Nicky?"

Lauren nodded.

"I think you've had a very lucky escape, Lauren. Now that we know who she is, we can find her and put a stop to this."

"She left because she believed me."

"Because you told her the truth."

Lauren was rocking back and forth, and the tears were now steadily flowing down her cheeks.

"It was the truth, but I've done something terrible."

"What?"

"I saved myself but at the expense of someone else."

"Someone else? What do you mean? Who?"

"I wasn't thinking about the consequences. I was worried about Mia. So I told Nicky. I told her everything."

"What did you tell her?"

"It was a cowardly thing to do, but I had to put my baby first, so I sacrificed her."

"*Who*?"

"Mrs. Diamond. She was a science teacher. I asked her to unlock the cupboard and told her what they had done to Alex, but it was ten long minutes before she finally came to unlock the cupboard and we discovered Alex's body. If she had come sooner…"

"Don't let her out of your sight," Mackinnon ordered as he walked past PC Worthington.

He headed outside, pulling his mobile phone out of his pocket and called Collins again.

"We've got a name," he said. "Nicola Brent. Known as Nicky. She is our killer. Her sister was the student who died of an asthma attack. She'd been locked in a cupboard by a group of students – Beverley Madison, Troy Scott and Joe Griffin."

"I'll try and find an address for her," Collins said.

"You better make it quick. I think we have another target."

"Another student was involved?"

"No, not a student. It's Mrs. Diamond, the headmistress. She used to be the science teacher when Alex and Nicky attended the school. Lauren Hicks has just told Nicky that Mrs. Diamond didn't unlock the cupboard as quickly as she could have. I think Nicky is going to go after her."

"We have Mrs. Diamond's address. I'll send someone round there straight away."

CHAPTER FORTY-FOUR

COLLINS RETURNED MACKINNON'S CALL LESS than two minutes later. "Bad news. She isn't at home. Her husband answered the landline and told me she was working late. I got her mobile number from her husband, but she isn't answering."

"So we think she is still at the school?"

"Yes. She's catching up on some paperwork according to her husband. We are mobilising a team to get to the school now."

"I'm not far away," Mackinnon said. "I'll check it out now."

"All right, but if you see anything out of the ordinary, don't go rushing in, Jack. Wait for backup. There will be units on the scene shortly, so don't do anything stupid."

Mackinnon shook his head as he hung up the phone and stuffed his mobile back in his pocket. By the way Collins spoke, it sounded like he thought Mackinnon *tried* to get into trouble.

When Mackinnon arrived outside St George's, it was already dark, and the school gates were locked. A gust of wind blew swirling leaves around his feet.

Everything seemed quiet from where he stood. The school playground was empty and he couldn't even see any lights on in the school building. Perhaps Mrs. Diamond had already left.

He pressed the button on the intercom which stood beside the locked gate, but there was no answer. He walked around the perimeter, trying to find the car park, and sent Collins a text, asking for Mrs. Diamond's license plate number. If her car was there, Mackinnon decided he would go looking for her.

His phone beeped with an incoming text message.

Sandra Diamond – LM60 SMR

The gates around the car parking area weren't as sturdy or as high as the ones by the main entrance. Mackinnon could clearly see a solitary car left in the car park. But from where he stood, he couldn't see the number plate clearly.

He hesitated for a moment and then decided to try and scale the fence. It was harder than it looked. And when he finally heaved himself to the top of the fence, he lost his balance and tumbled over the other side, ripping his shirt in the process.

After dusting himself down, he walked forward, cautiously, towards the red car. When he was a few feet away he saw that it was without a doubt Sandra Diamond's car.

He scanned the outside of the building for any lights or signs of occupation, but all the windows were dark.

Ahead of him there were a set of blue doors and he walked towards them. He gave them a shove and was surprised when they opened.

He stepped inside the school and made his way along a corridor lined with green metal lockers. At the end of the hallway he stopped for a moment and listened.

He could hear a distant dripping sound as if a tap hadn't been fully turned off or something was leaking, but he couldn't hear voices.

He continued forward along the corridor, heading for the centre of the school.

CHAPTER FORTY-FIVE

SANDRA DIAMOND SIGNED THE LAST letter on her desk with a flourish, then sighed and leaned back in her chair.

Thank goodness that was over. There was only one more thing she had to do this evening before she could go home.

She manoeuvred the mouse, clicking on her admin folders and locating a template file on her PC. It was a letter to parents, reminding them of the strict dress code at St George's.

A number of the girls had taken to wearing skintight trousers because the last letter she had sent out hadn't expressly forbidden them. They thought school was some kind of fashion show. Honestly, she had hoped that the parents would have had a little common sense.

Sandra Diamond shook her head as she made adjustments to the template letter. Changing the date and adding an extra line about the skintight trousers, she scowled in annoyance.

Her fingers paused above the keyboard when she thought she heard a noise outside in the corridor. She waited for a moment, listening out for anything unusual, but there was nothing. It must have been her imagination.

It was always strange to be in the school after hours. The place was so full of life during the day, and so noisy when it was full of children. The quiet at this time of night seemed almost spooky.

She adjusted her glasses and read through the Word document. That should do the trick, she thought. At least until some other way of dressing came into fashion. It had been platform shoes a few years ago. Now, that had been really ridiculous. The girls were constantly tripping over things.

She clicked on the print option from the file menu and printed off a copy of the letter. She selected the printer in the secretary's office next door, so that the following morning the secretary would be able to photocopy the letters and stuff them in envelopes. The children could take them home at the end of the day.

A shrill beep, signalling a paper jam, came from the printer.

The noise made Sandra jump.

"For goodness sake," she muttered under her breath.

She had worked here for years and had grown used to the place, but she had never liked working late here alone.

When she'd originally decided to be a teacher she thought it was going to be brilliant having all the summer holidays off and finishing work at three thirty every day. How wrong she was.

At least she got out of the marking these days. She used to really hate that. It had been soul destroying going over all the science papers and realising just how little her students paid attention.

She had come to St George's fresh out of teacher training college, full of exuberance, thinking she was going to make a difference to all the young lives. Her enthusiasm had lasted approximately six months.

Sandra didn't really know why she had stayed at St George's for all this time. Perhaps it was because she thought she wouldn't be good at anything else. She had planned to move on, but those plans had never come to fruition, and now she was almost at retirement age and had only ever worked at St George's.

At least she had been promoted. She had worked her way up through the teaching ranks and ten years ago, she achieved the position of headmistress. That had been a disappointment too.

Sandra got up from the desk and wandered outside into the school secretary's office.

The lights were off, but Sandra could see the red flashing light on the printer.

She considered leaving it until tomorrow morning, but then she would have to deal with dirty looks and snide comments from the secretary. She sighed and pulled open the paper drawer. She leaned over and tried to peer inside. She couldn't see a paper jam. The stupid thing was just temperamental. It seemed to have a mind of its own.

She yanked the whole drawer free from the printer and

reached inside. Nothing. There didn't appear to be any paper stuck in the mechanism.

Groaning with frustration, she reached down to switch the printer off at the plug, and out of the corner of her eye, she thought she saw a movement.

Sandra flinched and stared through the door out into the corridor beyond. The door had a small pane of glass, but it was misted and the corridor was dark.

Sandra eased herself up slowly to a standing position and then took a step towards the door. She was letting her imagination run away with itself. It was time to go home. She would leave the stupid printer until tomorrow. Hopefully the secretary would sort it out without making a tremendous fuss.

Sandra quickly walked back into her office and grabbed her handbag and jacket together with a yellow folder full of notes that she was supposed to look over before tomorrow's Governors' meeting.

She locked the door to her office and walked back through the secretary's area, looking nervously around her. Before she closed the door to the secretary's office, she reached out and fumbled for the light switch on the wall. As the lights flickered on and illuminated the corridor, Sandra could see the row of uniform lockers under the stark fluorescent lighting. The familiar sight made her relax.

She quickly locked the door to the secretary's office and strode off in the direction of the car park. She was already late for dinner and George would be moaning. He'd retired two years ago, but that didn't mean he ever thought to make the dinner himself. He didn't bother with the housework either, instead keeping himself busy by playing golf.

Sandra stepped through the double doors exiting the school and shivered. The cold December air hurt her chest as she breathed it in. The weather had changed suddenly this week and winter had hit England full force.

Sandra walked towards her red Ford Focus and pressed the key fob on her key ring to unlock the car. There was a beep and the lights flashed. Sandra had just opened the boot and put her handbag and the yellow folder inside when she heard a buzzing noise.

Her phone. She must have forgotten to take it off silent after her meeting this afternoon. Sandra propped her bag up on the boot and started to rummage around inside it when a voice close behind her made her freeze.

She felt something hard pressed against the small of her back.

"Hello, Mrs. Diamond. It's been such a long time."

CHAPTER FORTY-SIX

I FORCED MRS. DIAMOND TO go back into the school and led her into the very classroom where it had happened. I secured her wrists behind her back, using green gardening twine, then bound her ankles.

I also decided to use a gag, not that she had tried to scream. I just felt it was appropriate.

But as I stepped back to admire my handiwork, I had an uneasy feeling.

I didn't like what I saw.

Mrs. Diamond's face was heavily lined. She pleaded with me with her bloodshot eyes. She looked so much older than I remembered her. She didn't look scary or powerful, not like she had looked then.

"Please," Mrs. Diamond said, her voice muffled by the gag.

I loosened the strip of fabric I'd used as the gag.

"Please, don't hurt me. You can take what you want.

There's money in my handbag, and there are new computers in one of the classrooms down the hall. You could take them and leave. Probably get quite a bit of money for them and I would never tell anyone. I'd say I never saw your face."

I held up a hand to silence her and stop her babbling. "I'm not a thief, Mrs. Diamond."

I ignored her and walked about the classroom, taking it all in. The school had been modernised since I had been a pupil here. The decor was all different, bright colours instead of the institutional grey we'd had. The layout was the same, though, and the cupboard was in the same place.

I moved forward, tested the handle and smiled. It was unlocked. Inside there were stacks of Bunsen burners and rows of gleaming glassware. I picked up a measuring cylinder and inspected it. It was new, good quality stuff. Not like the chipped, battered equipment we used to use.

I walked back into the classroom and was gratified when Mrs. Diamond flinched as I passed within a few inches of her.

If she was scared of me now, that was nothing to how petrified she was going to feel in a few minutes.

I stopped in front of her and leaned back to perch on one of the desks. "Well, Mrs. Diamond, do you recognise me?"

Mrs. Diamond shook her head and her greying curls bashed against her cheeks.

"I'm hurt," I said, tilting my head and giving her a smile. "I've never forgotten you. How could I?"

She was really scared now and shaking uncontrollably.

"Well, I won't hold it against you. You can still have

your present. Just wait until you see what I have in this bag."

I moved the black holdall so it was on the ground between us, and I inched open the zip.

Mrs. Diamond's eyes were fixed on the bag. She was breathing rapidly. I thought she might hyperventilate or have an asthma attack — wouldn't that be sweet justice?

But Mrs. Diamond was made of sterner stuff than I thought. Her eyes remained locked on the holdall as I finished unzipping the bag.

I didn't reach inside. I didn't have a death wish. Not yet anyway. Instead, I held the bottom of the thick black canvas and tilted it, encouraging the occupant to emerge.

When the smooth brown snake slithered out of the bag, Mrs. Diamond's reaction didn't disappoint me. She screamed and writhed, desperate to get away from the snake.

Even though her ankles were tied together, she managed to propel herself backwards with her heels, sliding along the floor. I watched her with interest. I hadn't bothered to replace the gag. There was no need. There was nobody here to hear her scream.

She seemed to be sufficiently terrified, so I thought it was time for the next step.

I bent down beside her, and although she tried to move away from me, she couldn't, and I yanked her hair, keeping her head in position.

I leaned close to whisper in her ear. "I think I should tell you what this is all about," I said, but I knew Mrs. Diamond already understood.

She'd been lying when she said she didn't recognise me.

She must have heard the news and realised something was wrong when her ex-students started dropping like flies. Even though the press had picked up the wrong end of the stick and had no idea why I was doing this, I knew that Mrs. Diamond would.

"It wasn't my fault," she blurted out. "You can't hold me responsible for what happened to your sister."

I felt a shiver of repulsion for the old woman. "Yes, I can. It all started with you. You made her stand up in front of the whole class and give a talk, even though you knew she'd be ridiculed and teased afterwards."

"I was trying to help. She needed to toughen up," Mrs. Diamond said and then licked her lips. "It was those awful children. I didn't have any idea they would lock her in a cupboard. How could I?"

"Her school bag was on her desk," I said in a whisper and walked away from her, staring out of the dark window. "Did you know that? Her inhaler was just feet away in her bag. It could have saved her."

Behind me, I heard Mrs. Diamond sob, and I hated her for it. She was the one that needed to toughen up now.

I heard a high pitched squeal, and when I turned around, I saw that the snake was moving towards Mrs. Diamond, its tongue flickering out and tasting the air.

I smiled as I watched it slither towards her. Perhaps I wouldn't have to use the syringe this time.

"Please... Please, make it go away. You've got it all wrong. I was the one who found her. I called the ambulance. I did everything I could to save her."

I sat down on top of one of the desks and stared at her.

The snake had stopped its approach, but its tongue continued to flicker out, looking for prey.

"I know that's not true. Lauren Hicks came to find you. She told you that Alex was locked in a cupboard. You could have come to help her straight away, but instead you told her that you needed to finish your coffee first."

Mrs. Diamond shook her head in horror. "No! That's not what happened."

"Are you telling me that Lauren Hicks lied?"

"No, not lied exactly, but she was only a child. She must have gotten things confused."

I gave her a scathing look.

"It was only a couple of minutes, and then I helped her. It wasn't my fault. I thought it was just a prank."

I gripped the side of the desk hard.

Mrs. Diamond threw her head back and screamed.

CHAPTER FORTY-SEVEN

MACKINNON LOOKED UP. HE COULD have sworn he heard a woman scream. He froze in the corridor, listening.

Sandra Diamond's office had been locked and there was no evidence of a disturbance as far as he could see. He had considered breaking down the door just in case, but he was pretty sure it was empty. He didn't fancy ending up with a bruised shoulder and the bill for a broken door if Sandra Diamond had got a lift home tonight with someone else.

The only thing that seemed out of the ordinary was the printer in the secretary's office. The paper jam light was flashing, and the drawer had been removed, but that was hardly cause for alarm.

He heard the scream again, louder this time, and broke into a run, heading towards the noise. He had only gone a few paces, to the end of the corridor and turned the corner, when he ran into a solid wall of flesh.

He was cracked over the head with something hard, and

then before he could hit out and react, he felt a solid mass propel him to the floor.

Mackinnon twisted his torso and pushed back hard. A light flashed in his eyes momentarily dazzling him.

He managed to get the upper hand on his attacker by pushing hard upwards and flipping his assailant over.

There was a grunting sound beneath him as the attacker made contact with the floor. Mackinnon put his forearm against the man's throat, using his body weight to pin him to the floor.

As the torch clattered out of the man's hands, Mackinnon saw that he was face-to-face with a grey-haired man of around sixty.

"I've called the police," the man said in a strangled voice because Mackinnon was still resting his arm on his windpipe. "You won't get away with this."

Who on earth was this? Mackinnon rocked back on his heels, loosening his grip.

"I *am* the police," he said.

The man looked at him doubtfully, and with a sigh, Mackinnon wrenched his warrant card from his pocket and showed the man his ID.

"Well, why on earth didn't you say so in the first place?" The man sounded indignant.

Mackinnon wanted to point out that he hadn't exactly been given the opportunity to introduce himself, but he didn't want to waste time arguing.

"I heard somebody call out," Mackinnon said. "It sounded like a woman screaming."

The man sat up and nodded. "Me too."

"Do you work here?"

Another nod. "I'm the caretaker."

"Did you really call the police?"

The man hesitated and then shook his head. "No, I was only bluffing."

"Okay. It doesn't matter. More officers are on the way. Go into one of the offices or classrooms and lock the door if you can."

Without waiting for an answer, Mackinnon took off heading in what he hoped was the right direction. He'd only travelled a few feet when he heard voices.

"Oh, God, please no. Please, make it stop."

They were in the classroom just off the main corridor. The desperation in the woman's voice meant that Mackinnon didn't hesitate. It might have been wise to wait for backup, but the sheer terror of thinking that might be too late caused Mackinnon to wrench open the door.

When he burst into the room, he saw Sandra Diamond sitting on the floor. Her hands and feet were tied and what had been a gag hung loosely around her neck.

A tall slim woman sat on one of the desks. She smiled at Mackinnon as he entered.

"Police," Mackinnon said.

"You are too late," Nicola Brent said and then her gaze shifted to the floor.

Mackinnon didn't dare take his eyes off Nicola Brent when he said, "Are you okay, Mrs. Diamond?"

It was a ridiculous question. She clearly wasn't okay. She was tied up and almost hysterical.

Mackinnon made a move towards her to loosen the restraints when he suddenly saw her reason for distress. A three-foot long snake with black circular markings on its back was steadily slithering towards her. Mackinnon recoiled.

"Put that thing away now," he ordered, but Nicola Brent just stared at him.

"You can stop this now, Nicky. She hasn't been hurt, and I know you don't really want to hurt her. This isn't about Mrs. Diamond. This is about your sister," Mackinnon said. "I know you think she has been forgotten but she hasn't."

"She has to know how it feels," Nicola said, her voice devoid of emotion. "You should leave now. I don't want to hurt you."

Something resembling remorse flashed across her face. "How is that detective? The one with the grey hair?" She shook her head. "I didn't mean to hurt him, but I had to do it. He was going to ruin everything."

Mackinnon took a deep breath. He couldn't think straight when there was a venomous snake only a few feet away from him. What had Claude said about striking distance? He wished he had paid more attention.

"He is still in hospital."

"I thought I'd killed him."

Sandra Diamond began to moan softly as the snake shifted position.

"No one did anything for Alex," Nicola Brent said. "You should have helped her. You were the adult." Nicola was talking to Sandra Diamond, but she was too focused on the snake to pay her any attention.

"Someone should have stopped them. Someone should have brought the bullies to account, but no one did anything for her."

"You did," Mackinnon said.

Nicola Brent looked up, surprised. "Yes." She smiled. "I made them pay."

"You did," Mackinnon said. "But no one else needs to get hurt now. You've made your point. You can see how scared Mrs. Diamond is. She understands. She is sorry."

Mackinnon took a step forward towards Nicola. He could see the black bag and figured perhaps if he could throw it over the snake, it might stop moving. That could be a naive hope, but he had to try.

"It's over now, Nicola," he said and took another step forward.

Then he saw what she held in her hand.

She had slowly pulled it out of her pocket and held it in front of her.

The syringe.

No doubt full of the same venom that had killed Beverley Madison, Joe Griffin and Troy Scott.

In that moment, Mackinnon's senses seem to be heightened. He could see the glistening drop of liquid on the tip of the needle.

"Nobody else has to die," Mackinnon said. "It's over."

The snake passed within an inch of Mrs. Diamond's leg and she was shaking almost convulsively.

Mackinnon heard the welcome sound of police sirens in the distance. It wouldn't be long until officers were swarming the building.

"You need to put the syringe down now, Nicola. You've done enough."

Nicola Brent hesitated. Her lower lip trembled and then she slowly leaned down and placed the syringe on the floor.

Only seconds later, police officers burst into the room behind Mackinnon.

"Watch out for the snake!" Mackinnon yelled.

Two officers cuffed Nicola Brent as Mackinnon leaned down beside Mrs. Diamond and started to untie her restraints.

Her wrists were marked with red grooves, one so deep it had drawn blood.

"You're going to be okay now," Mackinnon said. "She didn't inject you before I got here, did she?"

Mrs. Diamond managed to shake her head, but she seemed incapable of speech.

A uniformed officer that Mackinnon didn't recognise entered the room with a long pole, prodding and poking the corners of the room, clearly looking for the snake.

Mackinnon helped Mrs. Diamond to her feet.

"Ambulance is outside. It just arrived," one of the uniformed officers told them as they left the classroom. He seemed very reluctant to go inside. "Have they found the snake yet?"

Mackinnon shook his head, and the officer shivered. "I better get someone from the animal unit in. I'm glad it's not my job to find it."

CHAPTER FORTY-EIGHT

OUTSIDE ON THE SCHOOL PLAYGROUND amidst the blue flashing lights, Mackinnon met up with Collins. They watched in silence as Sandra Diamond was treated by the paramedics for shock.

"She was lucky," Collins said after they closed the ambulance doors. "Shock and a few bruises. It could have been so much worse."

Mackinnon watched his breath form small white puffs in the freezing air.

"Did you hear the latest on Tyler?" Collins said. "It looks like he's going to be okay. Back to normal. At least as normal as Tyler ever can be."

Mackinnon managed a smile. "Thank God."

Nicola Brent was led past them in handcuffs to a squad car. She didn't look back.

"She doesn't look like she is capable of killing anyone," Collins said and he shook his head. "I should have learned by now that it's normally the person you would least expect."

"Do we know what triggered it?" Mackinnon asked. "I mean, what happened to her sister was years ago, so why now?"

"We found out she's been looking after her mother for the past few years. Her mother has dementia and her condition has declined rapidly in the last year. She got taken into a care home last week. I'm no psychologist, but I think that was probably the trigger."

Mackinnon ran a hand through his hair. "Fancy a drink after we're done here?"

"Go on then. I'll buy you a pint. I think we've earned it."

CHAPTER FORTY-NINE

MACKINNON WINCED AS SARAH SLAMMED her bedroom door. It had been over a week since Nicola Brent had been apprehended. Despite the sensational news coverage of the Charmer during the investigation, the papers and the news programmes on television were surprisingly quiet about the actual arrest.

The previous week had been filled with paperwork and form filling. Dotting the i's and crossing the t's and getting everything ready for a watertight case for the CPS.

It was the Saturday before Christmas, and Mackinnon sat on one end of the sofa with Katy at the other.

Katy had her feet curled up under her and was engrossed with something on the iPad. Technically, the iPad belonged to Chloe, but with Katy and Sarah using it she never seemed to get a look in.

Katy wasn't yet back to her normal lively self, but now that plans had been put in place for her to attend a new school next term, she was definitely happier than she had been before. Sarah was a different story.

The plane ticket her father was supposed to be sending her for Christmas hadn't materialised. In fact, he hadn't even bothered to ring her yet, and there was only a few days until Christmas. Instead of blaming her father, Sarah took it out on her mother, storming about and generally making everyone miserable. She was only back for three weeks over the Christmas holidays. Mackinnon felt guilty, but for him those three weeks couldn't pass quickly enough.

Just before Sarah had returned home for Christmas, Mackinnon had received a late-night phone call from her. She'd been drunk and had run out of money, so she couldn't afford a cab home. Mackinnon had driven across to Kingston from Derek's place in Hackney to pick her up outside a nightclub.

He tried to tell her she needed to be more responsible and tried to explain why it was so dangerous to get into that sort of situation. That had just earned him a sulky glare.

He hadn't even mentioned the incident to Chloe. She had enough on her plate at the moment, trying to solve Katy's bullying problem.

Mackinnon had just reached for the remote control to switch the channel, when there was a knock at the front door. Katy didn't budge. She didn't even look up from the iPad.

"I'll get it then, shall I?" Mackinnon said, getting to his feet.

When he opened the front door, he was surprised to see

Derek standing there. Mackinnon stepped back to let him in and then he noticed what Derek was carrying.

"What on earth?"

Derek grinned and held up the largest turkey Mackinnon had ever seen. "You haven't got one yet, have you?"

Mackinnon managed to shake his head.

From behind him he heard Chloe say, "Nice to see you, Derek, come in. Jack, shut the door. It's freezing."

Mackinnon shook his head as Derek walked past him, holding the turkey by the neck.

"That bird could probably feed twenty people," he said. "And it's not even plucked."

Derek shrugged. "It's organic," he said as if that explained everything.

"I've brought you a turkey," Derek said proudly to Chloe as he walked into the kitchen and waggled the bird's head.

Mackinnon followed Derek into the kitchen just in time to see the look of shock on Chloe's face.

"Oh...How kind." She shot Mackinnon a worried look. "Where are we going to keep it?"

Luckily Chloe had a spare fridge they kept in the garage, and Mackinnon just managed to fit the bird in there.

When he returned to the kitchen, Derek was leaning back on the kitchen counter, cradling a mug of coffee.

"It didn't work out," he said. "It was just one of those things." He shrugged and looked glumly down at his coffee.

Mackinnon guessed he was telling Chloe about his recent split.

"Oh, you poor thing," Chloe said sympathetically and then handed Mackinnon his cup of coffee.

"What are you going to do about Christmas?" Chloe asked. "You were planning to spend it with Julia, weren't you?"

"Oh, I don't know," Derek said, putting on a hangdog expression. "I'll be all right. I'll just spend the day watching telly on my own."

"Nonsense. You should spend Christmas with us, shouldn't he, Jack?"

Mackinnon had to grin at the beaming smile on Derek's face. It was quite obvious he had been angling for an invite, which was why he had brought the turkey.

"You're welcome to have Christmas dinner with us, mate," Mackinnon said. "On one condition."

Derek's forehead puckered in a frown and he immediately looked suspicious.

"What condition?"

"You help me pluck that turkey!"

CHAPTER FIFTY

CHRISTMAS EVE WAS MACKINNON'S LAST day of work before Christmas. After a heavy day of paperwork, the MIT team had headed to the Red Herring for a drink after work. The pub was packed and it seemed that everyone had had a similar idea.

Tinsel decorations hung around the windows, and there were free mince pies laid out on the bar.

Charlotte was getting into the Christmas spirit by drinking mulled wine, but Mackinnon turned his nose up and ordered a Speckled Hen.

Tyler was holding centre court. He had been released from hospital only yesterday, and Mackinnon was pretty sure his doctors wouldn't have approved of him heading straight to the pub the day after. Most of his bandages had been removed and he only had a small one now at his right temple. The doctors had needed to shave off his hair, but it had already started to grow back in grey tufts.

"The next round is on me," Tyler said.

"You can tell he's had a bang on the head," DC Webb said loudly as he cackled into his fourth pint.

"Ha bloody ha," DI Tyler said. "You better make the most of my generosity. I'll be back to my miserable self after Christmas."

Tyler handed over a couple of twenty pound notes to DC Collins, who went up to the bar to order the drinks.

Mackinnon leaned to his right until he was close to Tyler, and when nobody else could hear him, he said, "It's good to have you back."

Tyler looked at him with a smirk on his face. "Do you know, I could almost believe you meant that."

Mackinnon grinned. It was good to have the team complete again.

DC Collins brought back the drinks from the bar and handed them out. Everyone raised their glasses, and they toasted Tyler's health.

Tyler got to his feet.

"Oh, no, someone stop him. He's going to give a speech," DC Webb shouted out.

Charlotte slapped DC Webb on the arm. "Shut up!"

"No, I'm not, you cheeky so-and-so." Tyler lifted his pint. "I just want to wish everyone happy Christmas."

Everyone raised their glasses again and said in chorus, "Happy Christmas."

Tyler sat back down, looked around at everyone chatting and laughing and felt a warm glow. He was in danger of going soft.

The nurse who'd removed his bandages yesterday had told him he'd been one of their most popular patients. He'd had visitors every day he had been in hospital. Everyone from the team had taken the time to come and see him even though he was out for the count. Even DC Webb.

He grinned and raised a glass at DC Collins, who was launching into his famous story about Mackinnon and the Yucca plant.

Evie Charlesworth was giggling uncontrollably as Charlotte told DC Webb off for saying something inappropriate to one of the bar staff.

Tyler relaxed back in his chair. This year hadn't been his best.

His marriage had gone down the toilet, and he didn't have any family to speak of, but he was lucky to be alive, and he was very lucky to have this lot as friends. He hoped next year would be a good one for all of them.

THANK YOU!

THANKS FOR READING DEADLY PAYBACK. I hope you enjoyed it!

I am currently working on the next book in the Deadly Series. If you would like to be one of the first to find out when my next book is available, you can sign up for my new release email at www.dsbutlerbooks.com/newsletter

Reviews are like gold to authors. They spread the word and help readers find books, and I appreciate all reviews whether positive or negative. If you have the time to leave a review, I would be very grateful.

You can follow me on Twitter at @ds_butler, or like my Facebook page at http://facebook.com/d.s.butler.author

The next book in the series is Deadly Game. Turn the page to read the first chapter.

DEADLY GAME EXTRACT

Benny Morris stood in front of the Rose Hill Community Centre, shuffling from foot to foot impatiently.

They were late.

"Late, late, late," Benny muttered, slapping his hands together and stamping his feet.

A man walking past gave him a startled look and then hunched his shoulders, fixing his eyes on the ground and giving Benny a wide berth.

Benny was used to people keeping their distance. His size made people go out of their way to avoid him. At six foot five and eighteen stone, Benny Morris was a big man. His brother, Rob, told him his size was something to be proud of because it made people respect him and think twice before taking liberties.

An elderly woman walking towards him with a shopping trolley took one look at him and crossed to the other side of the road.

Benny waved and grinned at her, a nice big smile, showing all his teeth, but that just made her scurry away faster.

Rob, said he shouldn't worry about people like that, but he couldn't help it. He wanted people to like him.

He looked down at his freshly polished shoes. Shiny shoes were important to Benny. His trousers swung around his ankles because he kept pulling his trousers up too far. Rob told him off for doing it and said he looked like a simpleton, but Benny wanted to have his trousers high up on his waist, just like he wanted to have shiny shoes.

He looked at the Star Wars watch strapped to his wrist and muttered to himself again, "Late, late, late."

He looked in the direction the girls normally came from, past the Fried Chicken Palace and the bus stop. He saw the girls every morning, and they were normally here by now.

Rob wasn't going to be happy. Benny bit his lip as he imagined his brother's reaction.

He wasn't usually allowed to work with his brother.

"Don't blow this Benny," Rob had said that morning. "There'll be big trouble if you do."

He knew exactly what would happen if he did mess up. They wouldn't go to McDonald's for tea, and Benny wouldn't get his present.

He'd had his heart set on getting a new Xbox for ages, and Rob had promised to get it for him just as long as he brought the girls to the alleyway behind Celandine Gardens.

Benny bounced on the balls of his feet. "Come on, come on," he muttered.

He wished they would hurry up. The sooner they got

here, the sooner he could have his Xbox. He grinned. If he was really lucky, his brother might even have time to get the Xbox today. He could spend the whole afternoon playing online.

He smiled and waved to a little boy who walked past with his mother.

The little boy waved back, but his mother yanked on the boy's hand before quickly crossing to the other side of the road.

Benny sighed.

His brother didn't like to be kept waiting. He'd probably get told off now.

The excitement of having a new Xbox faded. If his brother were really angry, he'd forget about Benny's present, and there would be no trip to McDonald's, either. It would be beans on toast for dinner. That's what happened last week when he'd done something wrong, and Benny hated beans. They were too little to stay on his fork.

He broke out into a broad grin when he saw the two girls walking towards him.

"Hello," he shouted out, unable to wait until they reached him.

He bounded over to them, and they both grinned at him.

He liked the girls. They'd been working in the centre for a few weeks. The staff changed a lot at the centre, and he'd never liked anyone as much as the two girls. They weren't scared of him. They taught him how to use computers, showed him funny YouTube videos on the Internet and told him how good the new Xbox was.

"Hi, Benny," they said in unison.

"What are you doing out here?" Ruby asked. "The centre should be open already. You can go in if you like."

Benny nodded. He knew that. He'd been coming to the centre for years before the girls had arrived. This morning was different. He had something to do.

He licked his lips and closed his eyes, trying to remember what he was supposed to say. He needed to get the words exactly right. Otherwise, he wouldn't get the Xbox.

"I need you to help me," he said. "I found a bag of puppies in Celandine Gardens. I didn't know what to do, so I left them there. Can you come and help me?"

"Oh, how horrible. How could somebody do something like that?" Lila said. She patted Benny's arm. "Let's go and get them."

"We can call the RSPCA," Ruby said.

Benny nodded and smiled even wider.

His brother would be proud of him. Things were going exactly to plan.

He hummed to himself as the girls chatted about a program that had been on telly last night.

"This way," he said confidently as he led them across the cobbled courtyard.

He stepped into the alleyway and turned back to smile at them again. "It's just down here."

He was so excited he wanted to run to the end of the alley, but he knew his brother wouldn't be happy if he did that. That wasn't part of the plan.

So he walked slowly, and the girls followed him.

After they'd been walking for a couple of minutes, Ruby said, "Hang on, Benny." She wasn't smiling anymore. "How much further is it? We're going to be late for work. Perhaps you should get the puppies and bring them back to the centre."

He shook his head. No. He couldn't do that. That wasn't the plan.

"Are you pulling my leg, Benny? Are you sure you found some puppies?" Lila asked, grinning at him.

Lila was his favourite. She was always telling jokes and making Benny laugh, and she even laughed at *his* jokes, which Rob said weren't funny and didn't make sense.

He turned back and gave the girls a sly smile. He hoped they wouldn't be angry when they found out he'd tricked them. He thought they would understand if he told them about the Xbox. He didn't mind sharing. They were welcome to use it any time they wanted.

He opened his mouth to tell them the truth when his brother's voice sounded at the end of the alleyway.

"Good job, Benny. You'd better get yourself off home now."

He smiled, but when he turned back to the girls the smile slid from his face. They looked scared.

"It's all right," Benny said and started to explain about the Xbox, but his brother cut him off, and Benny saw another man step out of the shadows.

The man had a big nose and wore a baseball cap. He lunged forward, shouting and swearing, and Benny took a step back, not sure what to do.

He looked to his brother for help as he always did. Rob was clever and would know what to do, but his brother didn't say anything. He didn't even tell the man off for shouting at Benny.

One of the girls screamed, and the nasty man grabbed her by the throat.

Benny looked at them in horror. "No, don't hurt her. Let her go."

"Stay out of it," his brother ordered.

Benny's hands were shaking as he lifted them and pressed them hard against his ears to block out the sound of the girls' screams.

"No," he sobbed. "This wasn't the plan."

"Go home, Benny," his brother shouted at him.

Benny didn't like shouting. It scared him. He began to moan and shake his head.

The nasty man laughed as he punched Lila on the side of her head, and she fell to the floor in front of Benny.

"No!"

The man in the baseball cap turned to Rob and said, "He'd better come with us. The bloody fool will probably run off and tell somebody."

Benny watched in horror as the man put a hood over Ruby's head. She was wriggling, trying to escape when the man in the baseball cap punched her in the stomach.

Benny's lip wobbled. "Stop hurting her."

"Shut your gob and make yourself useful. Carry the other one," the man in the baseball cap snapped.

Benny looked down at the floor. Lila, the girl who'd laughed at all of his jokes, was laying motionless in front of him. There was blood on her lip.

Benny's eyes stung with tears as he looked at his brother for help.

"Come on, Benny," Rob said. "Pick her up."

Benny's hands were shaking as he leant down and

scooped the poor girl up. He lifted her as gently as he could, and her head lolled back against his arm.

With tears streaming down his face, he followed his brother and the man in the baseball cap.

Deadly Game is available now.

Deadly Obsession

Deadly Motive

Deadly Revenge

Deadly Justice

Deadly Ritual

Deadly Payback

Deadly Game

Lost Child

Her Missing Daughter

Bring Them Home

Where Secrets Lie

If you would like to be informed when the next book is released, sign up for the newsletter:

http://www.dsbutlerbooks.com/newsletter/

Written as Dani Oakley

East End Trouble

East End Diamond

East End Retribution

ACKNOWLEDGMENTS

To Nanci, my editor, thanks for always managing to squeeze me in when I finally finish my books!

I would also like to thank my readers on Facebook & Twitter for their entertaining tweets and encouragement.

My thanks, too, to all the people who read the story and gave helpful suggestions and to Chris, who, as always, supported me despite the odds.

And last but not least, my thanks to you for reading this book. I hope you enjoyed it.